I0772868

THE TAMING OF THE RUDE

Donna McHugh

ISBN-13: 978-1-962168-88-5

In Memory

This book is in the memory of my mother Rachel, who went home to be with Jesus on March 21, 2024. You will forever be in my heart.

P r o l o g u e

Betsy scrubbed out a cup and poured hot water from her teakettle over the used tea bag. "Better dan nothin'." She grumbled and took a sip of the weak scalding drink, then glanced into the living room where her husband sat in a stupor.

"Thomas, get yer drunken, lazy behind out of dat chair or, so help me, I'm gonna snatch ya bald if'n ya don't move right now. And you stink like an old dog who done rolled in fresh cowpies! Little wonder everybody crosses da street when dey see us comin.' Change out of dose rank smellin' clothes."

Thomas raised his fists and started toward her. "Ya don't smell so purty yerself."

Betsy continued her tirade. "Yer as nasty as yer Pap and just as stupid! What a disgrace!"

Thomas glared at her. "Who died and left ya my boss?"

"Ya didn't say dat, did ya?" Betsy let out a stream of expletives that could've scorched the ears of any sea-faring sailor.

Thomas swung at her with both fists, but she grabbed him by the seat of his pants and back collar and tossed his skinny frame through the doorway. "I said get your behind dressed, and I meant it. Now git! Make yerself decent-like. NOW!"

He slammed the bedroom door so hard that a piece of plaster fell from the ceiling and landed, unnoticed among the rest of the dirt and grime on the floor.

Time to get da snot-nosed kids up.

Betsy went to the bottom of the stairs and yelled their names out at the top of her lungs. Then, she thundered up the steps like an angry Mama bear and tossed the thin, ragged covers off them. "Didn't ya hear me callin' ya? Now ya'll kids better be downstairs in ten minutes or else."

"Mama, Kaylee wet the bed again," Jenny yawned.

Betsy grabbed her youngest girl by the arm and yanked her into the bathroom. "Strip," she demanded as her little girl bowed her head.

"Sorry Mommy." Kaylee cried and shivered as Betsy scrubbed her naked little body in cold tap water while impatient knocks sounded on the door. She grabbed a threadbare towel and hoisted her to her arms. "I'm comin' just hold yer horses." She unlocked the door as the rush of impatient children nearly bowled her over. "Take it easy, will ya?"

She dug through the so-called dresser for underclothes for her little girl, then tossed a wrinkled outfit on the bed. "Get dressed," Betsy growled then stomped downstairs.

She went to the rough-and-ready kitchen to find something to eat for the family. She sighed. *Bread and jelly again. Wish I cud do better dan dat, but money's scarce as hen's teeth. What little I make workin' my tail off pays for da 'lectricity and 'portant stuff. Da gov'mint helps with food stamps, but Thomas always finds da card an' trades food for alcohol.*

She took the crust and smeared it with a thin layer, leaving the rest of the loaf for her children.

If'n dat man of mine did somethin' besides drink all day; we wouldn't be in dis mess. Dere ain't nothin' worse dan tryin' to feed all da young'uns off day-old bread and gov-mint jelly.

She opened the outside door and a blast of frigid air hit her in the face. She looked around for the metal can on the porch. *Hope da neighbors cow made extra milk dis mornin'.*

She opened the lid and was not disappointed. *Good, at least we won't be hungry.*

After the children ate, they raced to the car pushing and shoving each other on the way.

Dere some wild ones, dey are.

She clumped toward the bedroom yelling at Thomas the whole way. She yanked open the door. "Come on. Yer gonna make us late and dat ain't happenin'." She found him lying out on the bed, snoring away.

"Life would be easier if I let ya sleep, but ya gotta be in church cuz of yer probation. Da judge went easy on ya for da DUI. One thing dat ain't happenin' is for ya ta slack off da church-goin'."

Thomas opened one eye and shut it again.

"Ok, sorry to do dis." She grabbed a glass of water and flung it at him.

"What'd I do, dis time?" Thomas wiped his face and scowled, "Ya make me so mad!" He raised his fists.

"Ya look so handsome now that your face is clean. And ya cain't hit me on a Sunday."

"Don't ya start bein' high and holy ta me. I get enough of dat from da preacher man."

"Come on." She shoved his ratty shoes on. "We're goin' ta church."

1 Trouble in Paradise

Betsy marched Thomas out to the car. "Get in." Turning to the children, she said, "Y'all better buckle yer seatbelts. We're goin' to church."

Betsy hopped into the driver's seat and turned the key in the ignition. *Click! Click! Click!*

She mumbled curses as she played whack-a-mole with every part under the hood. Betsy jumped in the driver's seat, pumped the gas pedal a few times for good measure, and talked sternly to it. "Crank over now, or I'm gonna hit ya again." The car coughed, sputtered, then purred like a kitten.

Betsy yanked the gearshift to reverse and backed down the driveway like the boogeyman chased her. She burned rubber as she turned out of the drive and sped toward the stop sign. "Anybody comin,' kids?"

"No!" They yelled.

She whipped the wheel to the right and drove across town like a NASCAR driver.

It wasn't long before squabbles assaulted her ears. She reached over the seat and swung her free arm in every direction.

"Ya missed me, na, na, nana, na, na."

"If'n ya'll don't stop, I'm gonna pull da car over and whop all ya'll's hides. Knock it off right now, or so help me, it won't be purty."

Kids in vehicles near the Freemans' car heard the threats. Faces plastered against the windows, eyes grew huge, mouths gaped as the cross words that stuck in their craw like fish bones. Silence reigned for an entire city block. Nobody wanted to tangle with that woman.

Finally, Betsy bounced into the church parking lot.

~

Pastor Johnson watched the commotion and took a deep breath as people scattered like billiard balls away from the cue to avoid being part of the Freeman Sunday Carnage.

One of these days, there's going to be a major accident in the parking lot. I can see the headline now. Community Church Pile-up. Many In Heaven Today.

Dear Jesus. Help me! He tried to calm his racing heart and then greeted the Freeman children as they charged through the entrance at full speed.

"Good morning, Peter, Hailey, Joseph, Jenny, and Kaylee." He extended his hand, but they blasted past him and bounced like bumper cars off furniture and parishioners alike.

Pastor Johnson called after them, but instant silence settled over the churchgoers. Every eye focused on the rogue youngsters as they raced to the second pew from the front. Mothers in their Sunday finest clothes clutched their children nearer.

Pastor Johnson heard the loud whispers breaking through the silence. "You better not act like those

Freeman hooligans, or you will be in deep trouble when we get home."

Then, the parents of the wild brood stormed in, slovenly dressed. The smell of stale beer and body odor swirled around them while their bitter words hung in mid-air. The ice queen herself, Betsy Freeman, stared at Pastor Johnson under her wild, tangled, red, frizzy bangs, daring him to say a word.

See what I mean, Jesus? They're scary. That's what I've been trying to tell You.

They're wounded people with problems like I deal with every day. Is there anything too hard for Me?

Well, no.

Good. They need a Savior, and I choose you to show Me to them.

Why try arguing with God? He always wins.

~

Betsy drug Thomas by his sleeve through the sanctuary door. "Come on, ya loser. Keep yer eyes open and big trap shut. Hey! Did ya see dat? What bout dat over dere? Help me out here." She hissed like a rattlesnake on caffeine.

Her children punched and tussled to be the first at her side with his or her bit of juicy gossip. Betsy kept busy writing things down while Thomas, her husband, stared off into the distance all bleary-eyed. "I know ya don't wanna be here, Thomas, but I'm keepin' yer hide outta jail. One of dese days ya will thank me."

"Puh! I would rather be sittin' at da bar with da guys dan listenin' to yer gossipin' waggly tongue."

And a Freeman fight broke out. Fists flew. Other parishioners skedaddled like rats from a sinking ship.

~

Pastor Johnson slipped into his office and gulped down two extra-strength headache pills, then made his way to the platform, and sat in his Reverend Chair. He looked around the sanctuary at the people gathered there. Then, his gaze fell on the happenings on the Freeman pew and his pulse sky-rocketed and chest tightened.

Breathe! He willed himself to calm down and shot another prayer heavenward.

What a messy bunch of people down there on that second pew. God, how are we to reach them? All they seem to do is distract, disrupt, and disrespect.

Did I not choose you to lead them in the right way?
Yeah, but...

Ah, ah, ah. No buts. Remember what happened to the Children of Israel when they questioned Me? You wouldn't want the ten plagues sent as a reminder, would you?

No, but I could use a few to settle the Freemans.
Chadwick Johnson!
Okay. I must go preach.

Pastor Johnson stood behind the pulpit and opened the Word of God. His sermon changed instantly to speaking about the plagues of the Egyptians. He hoped that the Freemans would listen and not disrupt his sermon, but not a chance.

As if on cue, partway through the worship service, they stood as one and clomped as loudly as a herd of circus elephants toward the restrooms. Body odor lingered behind them like the scent of spraying skunks. Ladies discreetly pulled hand fans from their purses and did a wave offering before the Lord as they walked by. Collectively, they inhaled and tried to not breathe. A thousand one...a thousand two... Once the Freemans tromped back in and resettled into the pew, the congregants put their fans away and drew in a fresh breath.

~

Every Monday, without fail, Pastor Johnson found a poorly written, venomous letter slid under his study door.

Preacher Man: Ya think yer so smart standin' up dere spoutin' off about what s'posed to be da Bible when we know ya made it up. Ya ain't fooled no one. We don't cotton ta da book learnin' and puttin' on airs. Just cuz ya got a bit of edjercation, don't mean ya know da first thing about preachin'. My grandpappy was a man of good ole horse sense. Ya ain't got enough to fill a hankey. Preach right or go away.

There was never a signature, but Pastor Johnson knew that it was from Betsy Freeman.

Finally, after weeks of harassment, Pastor Johnson called an emergency meeting of his Advisory Board. "We need to talk about the Freeman bunch. To quote one of the letters, 'Either I preach things their way or leave'." His eyebrows rose together, and his forehead wrinkled. "Look at these." Pastor Johnson handed out copies for them to read.

"Are you kidding me?" Darrell James disgustedly threw the papers onto the table. "Those foul-smelling bunch of ingrates!"

"Now, now! They may be all that, but Jesus loves

them anyhow." Pastor Johnson interrupted.

"Let's pray." Every head bowed and eyes closed as Frederick Howard started his boisterous and determined prayer. "Dear Lord God, Almighty, we at the Community Church have a problem. Now, we know that you are an eternal God from everlasting. The Freemans are not a difficulty for You. But we as human beings with finite minds need the wisdom to bring them to Jesus."

"Amen." Everyone else called out because otherwise, they'd be here 'til midnight, and the rest of them had places to go and people to see.

The next morning, the Teen Department leaders barged into his office. "Joseph and Hailey Freeman terrorize the Sunday School classes."

"How?" Pastor Johnson frowned.

"Last week they sat on the back row together. We tried to separate them, but it didn't work. They'd kick the back of the seats in front of them until the teens fell out of their chairs. Then they'd laugh. 'I see London. I see France. I just saw you purple underpants. Why don't ya go tell yer mama? Go ahead. I dare ya." They'd snicker, shout, and laugh through the lesson. Some kids, who we have worked with for years, told us plainly that they won't be back, so how are we going to reach them now?"

"Let's pray about the situation." Pastor Johnson bowed his head, and the ladies respectfully followed suit. "Father, love the Freemans through us. We need Your wisdom, or the Freeman kids are going to ruin the youth department. This problem is tough, but not as complicated as parting the Red Sea or feeding the five thousand. Amen."

The ladies stared at him as if he had lost his marbles.

Mrs. Clark cleared her throat. "We thought you might want to deal with this." She plunked a well-wrapped packet on his desk.

"What is it?" *Sniff!* The smell took him back to his high school days. The boys' bathroom reeked of it. *Marijuana.* "Where did you get this?"

"It fell out of Joseph's pocket before he rushed out the door last Sunday. We overheard him trying to sell it to some of the other boys. Would you like me to call my nephew who is a local police officer?"

"Yes. Have him meet me here in the office. Please have a seat, ladies. We will deal with this together."

Pastor Johnson could hear sirens blaring within moments of her call. A tall young man appeared with his hat in his hands. "Aunt Linda, you called?"

"Yes. You know how I keep my eyes open for anything out of the ordinary."

"That you do. You're a good citizen."

Pastor Johnson leaned forward and slid the packet across the desk. "This is why she called you."

"I see." He opened his notebook and furiously wrote as the ladies all talked at once.

"We need to catch him in the act of distribution to charge him. I'll be in touch, Pastor. Good day, ladies." He tipped his hat to them and turned to leave.

Later that afternoon, the elementary teachers barged into his office with their report about Peter, Jennie, and Kaylee.

"Kaylee tried to redecorate the classroom walls, door, desks, and floor. It took me hours to clean it up," complained Miss Marshall, the preschool class teacher.

"If she was my little girl, I'd..."

"Aren't you glad she isn't?" interrupted Pastor Johnson.

Miss Marshall was speechless.

"Well, that's nothing," huffed Mrs. Abbott, the fifth-grade teacher. "Peter took the craft scissors and chased the girls around the room last Sunday. You should have heard the screaming and yelling as the girls tried to avoid him. But it didn't stop him from shredding some of their clothes. We've dealt with a lot of angry mothers demanding that we pay for the ruined outfits. You know there's no money in the budget for that."

"Jennie is just as bad." Mrs. Butler, the third and fourth-grade group teacher, interrupted. "She's always teasing and bullying the other kids. Many times, I have caught her sticky little fingers digging in the offering plate. Mark my words. She's stealing from God!

"Can we kick them out of Sunday School for the sake of the other children? They've gone too far this time!"

The pastor rubbed his temples as the Freeman Headache swelled. *How can you say that someone could not attend? The church sign said, "Everyone welcome," and that included the Freemans.*

Then, one Tuesday morning, a bomb dropped with the ringing of his phone. Pastor Johnson's superior, Bishop Lawrence, was on the other line.

"Good morning. How nice to hear your voice. To what do I owe this pleasure?" He played with the pen in his hand.

"I am doing well. Thank you. This is not one of our friendly discussions. Some matters of significant importance have arisen." The bishop changed to a more serious note. "I am calling in my official capacity."

"Oh, dear. What is wrong?" The minister drew in a deep breath and steeled himself.

"An anonymous parishioner has brought several charges against you."

Pastor Johnson slowly exhaled and blinked back tears. "Why in the world would anyone want to do that?"

The church leader continued. "I must take this to the Credential Committee. You have a proven record of integrity, so my hope is that these accusations do not sully that."

Pastor Johnson began pacing the floor like a caged lion. "We've had a new family attending lately, and they've been troublemakers, but would they stoop this low?"

"I will find out. The Elder's Council plan to meet with you at the end of the week." The bishop reassured him.

"I would never do anything to bring a black mark upon the church, or the denomination."

"I believe you, but I must investigate this so I can clear your name. Trust the process, Chadwick."

"But... but..." Pastor Johnson stammered, then hung up the phone in a daze.

Ugh! The Freemans again! Nobody else in the church gives us any trouble. That family is like having an acute case of poison ivy. You get one site scratched and ten more break out.

James 1:3 for you know that the testing

of your faith produces steadfastness. 1

Is that what this is all about, God? Have I not proven my faith in You enough?

Trust Me, Chadwick. I know what I'm doing.

I can do nothing else.

Sit back and watch Me work out My plan.

The following Friday morning, Pastor Johnson and his Advisory Board met in the conference room before the Council Meeting. Nobody spoke. Tension was so thick you could cut it with a knife.

Soon, the church secretary escorted Bishop Lawrence and his entourage in. She closed the door and the awkwardness intensified to the level of a first blind date.

~

Bishop Lawrence walked to the lectern, opened his thick notebook, and cleared the frog out of his throat. "Good morning." His voice boomed like the sea waves crashing against the rocks. "I'm going to cut to the chase. Your minister has anonymous accusations filed against him. Thus, the formal investigation into these church matters."

"This here ain't right," Frederick Howard, one of the Advisory Board Members, blurted out. "You ain't gonna find anything in this trumped-up kangaroo trial. This is unfair to Pastor Johnson."

"Regardless of whether it is reasonable or not, we must deal with it." The bishop pulled out the denominational discipline. " Section 115.b. of the Conduct Code says, *if there is any accusation against a pastor, the Elder's Council requires an investigation. The bishop must relieve the pastor from his duties, which is not to be more than ten days. After which time, a meeting with the affected church, the accuser(s), and the pastor(s) will take place."*

"This is all kind of wrong." Frederick blurted again.

Bishop Lawrence ignored him.

"Any questions, Pastor Johnson?"

Stunned, the minister said with a dry mouth and a raspy voice. "No."

"Good. We need all your computer passwords and cellphone. If we find anything troublesome, we'll let you know."

"Ain't this intruding on the pastor's privacy?" Frederick interrupted again. How would you like someone doing that to you? Huh?"

Crickets!

Pastor Johnson shook his head to make the sudden dizziness go away. He wrote down the information and pulled his cellular phone out of his suit coat pocket.

Bishop Lawrence handed him another one. "We'll be in touch. God be with you."

Frederick looked at Pastor Johnson. *He's as white as a sheet.*

When the meeting adjourned, Pastor Johnson stood to his feet, then collapsed to the floor as blackness enveloped him.

"Pastor, come on wake up." Frederick shook him but there was no response. "Come on, guys, don't just stand there with your mouths hanging open, do something. We gotta get him to the hospital. NOW!"

Several men jumped into action and helped lift him into Frederick's SUV. They worried that someone had killed their pastor.

2 Da Preacher Man's Goin' Down

Beep! Beep! Bump! Unfamiliar voices. Then the awful odor of the ammonia capsule under his nose woke him up with a jolt. Pastor Johnson sat up abruptly on the gurney in the ER. "Where am I? What's going on?" He opened his eyes to the chaotic scene.

The medical team surrounded him like a football huddle.

"Big poke, here, buddy." The lab tech stuck a needle in his arm.

A doctor leaned over his bed and looked directly into his face. "I'm Dr. Bender, and you are at Rosamond Hospital. Do you remember what happened?"

"I was at the church in a meeting with my superior. How did I get here?"

"You fainted and Mr. Howard put you in his car and raced here. Do you remember that?"

"No."

"You've got a good-sized goose egg on the back of your head. We're sending you for a CT scan to make sure you don't have a brain bleed."

"K."

Two porters whisked him out of the cubicle and down the hall to Medical Imaging. "Breathe in and hold your breath. This won't take long."

Pastor Johnson watched the little Pac Man figure above his head. The cheeks on the little guy puffed out and he turned red. Thirty seconds later the figure turned green.

"You can breathe…"

Good. I'm glad that's over!

Whiz! Whirl! The bed moved back into the cubicle.

The nurse hooked the IV onto the bed's pole then put the blood pressure cuff on his arm and pressed the button.

Squeeze!

My arm's going to fall off if this thing keeps it up.

"Your blood pressure seems a bit high. 160/100." I'll let the doctor know. In the meantime, try to rest and we'll see if it will come back down."

"Is my wife around?"

"I'll check. Be right back."

In a moment, his wife, Deborah, popped through the closed curtains. "Hi, honey. Are you all right?" She leaned down and kissed him.

"I'm okay now with you at my side."

"Not so fast, young man," Dr. Bender piped up. "You'll need to stay with us for a few hours yet. Your blood pressure needs to settle down. The good news is that there is no bleeding on the brain. I'd recommend that you lay low for several days while you recover. A vacation would help."

"I'm on it." Deborah whipped out her phone and

got busy while her husband fell asleep.

~

Meanwhile, Bishop Lawrence sat at the table in the conference room of the church. Documents filled the table and spilled over onto every available space in the room. He rubbed his eyes and yawned. "We've been at this for three days. Has anyone found anything to substantiate the accusations against the pastor."

"NO!" Came the reply as the heads came up and eyes stared back at him.

"Okay. Stop what you are doing. This witch hunt is over. Whoever accused him lied, and this makes me terribly angry." He scowled and pounded his fist on the table. "Put everything away. We're done here."

On Sunday morning, Bishop Lawrence watched the congregants enter trying to figure out who had lied about the pastor. He didn't have to wait long because the Freeman family burst through the doors in a typical rude fashion.

You've got to be kidding me! THEM? I should have known. The council found nothing in the complaints to censure Pastor Johnson. He's an honorable man.

They, on the other hand, hop churches like frogs in a pond...never satisfied, always critical, and unhappy. A look in the mirror might show them as the problem instead of everyone else.

The bishop opened his Bible and studied the text again.

James 1: 23, 24 2.

23.For if anyone is a hearer of the word and not a doer, he is like a man who looks intently at his natural face in a mirror.

24.   For he looks at himself and goes away

and at once forgets what he was like.

Freemans to a T. How am I going to show them the error of their ways without being unkind?

He stood to preach the word of God to the congregation. The Freemans sat there noisily on the pew being a huge distraction to the rest of the people.

After the service, the church leader stood in the foyer and shook hands with the congregants. He shivered as the infamous Freemans bulldozed a path right to his side. "Hey, yer Highness. Can ya believe da stuff da pastor done? Da preacher man ought to go ta jail." Betsy bellowed above the noise of the others talking.

Bishop Lawrence ignored her, but the Freemans jostled him about like a teacup, ready to overflow and make a mess. He tried to remain calm. Hot words were on the tip of his tongue when God spoke to him.

James 1:19 Know this, my beloved brothers: let every person be quick to hear, slow to speak, slow to anger; 3.

But God...

You can draw more flies with honey than with vinegar.

But if I ignore her, she'll go away.

We're talking about Betsy Freeman here.

That's true. I'd better see what she wants. She's poking me in the chest now. She must be desperate to say something. Betsy's up in my face. He sucked in a deep breath.

"Scuse me, I'm talkin' ta ya. Don't ya go pretendin' I'm not here."

The bishop exhaled and took the next breath through his mouth. "Are you sure the pastor did all those things?"

Betsy put her fists on her hips and harrumphed loudly, "Do ya think I'm lyin' ta ya? I'm a good Christian woman. Dat preacher man's goin' down."

Oh, we'll see what happens at the Elder's Council in a few days. You plan to be there, right?"

"Ya betcha." Betsy opened the church door and charged down the sidewalk like a runaway locomotive.

Bishop Lawrence smiled. *Her basket of woven lies is going to unravel like a frayed sweater.*

~

Betsy punched Thomas awake. "Member what today is?"

"No." He opened one eye.

"It's when da preacher man's goin' down. Git up and put some rags on cuz we're gonna see him roasted like da taters we had last night."

"We had taters?"

"Of course, Stupid. Ya was too stinkin' drunk ta know what we had for supper. Don't matter. GIT UP!"

Thomas had no choice but to pull his achy hungover body out of bed. "Hope all dis is worth it ta ya."

"Whaddya mean by dat?"

"We caused dem a lot of trouble. Don't ya think we done enough testin' of his patience?"

"Course not."

"It might not turn out like ya want. Ya push some men too far and dey snap. Ya never know what's under da choir boy outfit." Thomas slipped his belt through the loops and stared at her.

"Whose side ya on, anyway?" Betsy huffed and slammed the screen door. "Let's go or we're not gonna see what happens."

When they arrived, a large group from the church

was already there. "Dere better not be people in our seat or so help me, I'll toss dere hides right out of dere. Everybody knows dat da front seats are for da Freemans."

"Uh huh," Thomas mumbled.

"Yes!" Betsy crowed as they slid across the row like they were Little Leaguers sliding into first base. "We made it. Dat's what matters." She looked at the clock on the wall. "It's time ta start da roastin'." Betsy rubbed her hands in glee and grinned from ear to ear. *Da preacher man's goin' down.*

Betsy watched as Bishop Lawrence went to the podium. *Dat big uppity-up don't scare me none. He messes with me, and he's goin' down too. Nobody wins against me.*

Betsy listened as Bishop Lawrence read the preacher's charges. "The first accusation says that Pastor Chadwick Johnson is preaching things that are not in the Bible. The complainant states that Hezekiah is not in the Scriptures. Council, in your opinion, is Pastor Johnson guilty of this charge?"

Harrison Porter answered, "He is not guilty. Hezekiah appears several times in the Holy Bible."

Betsy stood up. "Ya need ta prove it ta me. I ain't never seen dat name in da Bible I read."

Harrison replied. "2 Kings 16:20 And Ahaz slept with his fathers and was buried with his fathers in the city of David, and Hezekiah his son reigned in his place."4.

"Well, I didn't see dat before. Okay, I'll give dat one ta ya. What's next?"

Bishop Lawrence read the allegation. "Inappropriate contact with a minor. This is serious and could end Pastor Johnson's career as a minister. It could place him behind bars for many years. Council, do you find this charge credible?"

Harrison answered. "Bishop, we have a slide to show." When he pulled it up on the screen, the room erupted in laughter.

"Order, we cannot have this!" The dignitary pounded his fist on the lectern.

Everyone quieted.

"What's so funny?" Betsy blurted out. "Dat ain't his woman. Are all ya'll blind? Dat dere's a young hussy."

"No, it isn't." Pastor Johnson clarified. "That is my fourteen-year-old daughter, Vanessa. My, how she looks like her mother, don't you think?"

"How was we s'posed ta know?" Betsy huffed and stomped her foot. "Ya need ta tell people stuff."

Pastor Johnson came to Betsy and looked her in the eye. His quiet voice unnerved her. "Ask about things you don't understand. Don't drag people through the mud by assuming anything. It can lead to big trouble. If I chose to, both of you could be behind bars for defamation of character and libel."

"Ya ain't puttin' me in da clink for somethin' dat weren't my idee. Da missus done all dis, not me." Thomas interrupted.

"Shut yer mouth." Betsy belted him one.

Pastor Johnson continued after their ruckus. "I choose to forgive you for what you did because Jesus, my example, faced false accusations from the Jews, and He forgave them. What you meant for evil; God turned it for good. I got a much-needed vacation."

With the wind out of her sails, Betsy hung her

head.

"Happy now, woman? Dat dere choir boy done licked ya good." Thomas blurted.

Betsy heard Bishop Lawrence clear his throat. "The least you can do is apologize for lying about Pastor Johnson. He ended up in the emergency room last week because of it. Shame on you! What do you have to say for yourselves?"

Ain't no way I'm apologizin' in front of all dese people. He can wait til Jesus comes back for dat.

Oh no! Here comes Miz Pennington. When she's angry, she scares me ta death. Wonder what she wants.

Betsy swayed a little as she stared into the steely gray eyes of the saint of God. *Dey could stare holes through a brick wall. Now dey're gazing at me. Ouch! She done got a new attack. Why is her cane pressin' on my foot?* Betsy blinked twice as the pain increased. Miz Pennington hissed at her. "Apologize, now."

Stunned, Betsy did not say a word.

"Excuse me, I told you to apologize to the pastor." Her eyes narrowed like an angry cat.

"Ow! Stop it," Betsy yelled at her.

Miz Pennington locked her eyes.

She means business! "Okay, okay. I'm sorry for da problem we caused. We were testin' da preacher man's patience like da Bible says ta do."

"It does not say to impose on another person's good nature." Bishop Lawrence interrupted.

Betsy rolled her eyes.

"Apologizing wasn't so hard, now, was it?"

Betsy watched as Miz Pennington's cane landed squarely on Thomas's ragged shoe.

"Your turn." She stared into his bloodshot eyes.

"What kind of example are you for your children? Tsk. Tsk."

"Sorry." Betsy heard Thomas mumble.

I don't think she's gonna accept dat.

"What did you say, Sonny? My ears don't work so well. Say it again so I can hear you."

"Sorry," Thomas replied louder as the cane pressed hard on his foot.

"Don't you two ever pull a stunt like that again or you'll have me to answer to. Understand?"

They nodded numbly.

Betsy's ears rang as Bishop Lawrence bellowed. "This trial is adjourned." *Slam!* The notebook slapped shut as the sound echoed eerily.

Miz Pennington leaned over to Thomas and Betsy. "That means get out of here before something worse happens to the two of you." She turned and limped away.

"What about da preacher man goin' down? Huh? Seems ta me dat ya was da one who got down."

"Aw, shut yer trap if ya ain't got nothin' nice ta say."

3 This Is God's House

Early Sunday morning, well before church services began, several people met in the foyer to discuss the plan to catch Joseph Freeman in the act of selling marijuana. Mrs. Clark's nephew, Luke Wellington and his partner, Tim Gibbons, spelled out the plan for everyone to follow. "You boys stand over there. We will be hiding behind the display on this side. Pastor, you, and the others take your positions where you normally do. Don't act nervous. We're counting on ya'll."

~

The Freeman car bounced into the parking lot right on time. The younger children and Hailey bolted off toward the church. Joseph lumbered along. His bangs covered his eyes, and his knees popped out of his jeans.

When he entered the building, two boys in equally ragged clothes, called to him. "Hey um, Joseph, listen. Do you still have that stuff for sale today?"

"Shut up! Wanna get me in trouble? Dat's twenty bucks." Joseph snarled.

He whirled around to see Officers Wellington and Gibbons with cuffs dangling from their fingers. "This way, Joseph." Both grabbed his arms and swiftly ushered him into the men's restroom, out of sight of the families entering the building.

"Empty your pockets and put everything on the counter."

Joseph drew out candy bar wrappers, loose coins, and rubber bands. *If'n dey want ta charge me, dey have ta find it themselves.*

"Now, I need to do a pat-down just to make sure you aren't hiding anything." Officer Wellington declared.

"Nuh-uh. I got rights. Ya gotta have prob' cause." Joseph whirled but Officer Gibbons met him face to face.

"Okay. Miranda Rights are coming right up."

Joseph stood there stunned for a second, then tried to make a run for it, but Officer Wellington lifted him by the back of his collar like a cat carrying a kitten.

"Now, let's try this again." He growled as he pulled several baggies out of Joseph's pockets and laid them on the counter.

"Where'd ya get this stuff?"

"I ain't tellin' ya dat."

"If you want a chance at a plea deal, you'll talk."

Joseph glared at him. "I don't care what ya want. I ain't bein' a snitch."

"Okay then. You can talk ta da judge tomorrow. He has a way of getting the truth out of people. Turn around and put your hands behind your back. You are under arrest for having a controlled substance with intent to distribute. You have the right to remain silent…"

"Yeah, Yeah, blah, blah, blah." Joseph interjected.

"Let's go." Officer Wellington tugged on his handcuffs.

As the officers and Joseph came out of the restroom and headed toward the exit, Mr. and Mrs. Freeman burst through the church doors. "What's goin' on?" Betsy bellowed. "Get da cuffs off him right now."

Officer Gibbons replied calmly, "I'm sorry, ma'am, we can't do that. Joseph needs to come with us."

"What!" she exploded. "No one takes my baby away."

"Mom, just shut up! Yer makin' a scene." Joseph angrily bellowed.

"Calm down, Joseph. You don't want any more charges added on here."

Turning to Betsy, Officer Wellington calmly explained. "We arrested Joseph for drug possession with intent to distribute. It's a shame that he can't respect church premises."

"Twas planted by church kids. Dere always pickin' on my young'uns." Thomas garbled.

"Nope, I don't believe that for a minute." Officer Wellington pulled out a baggie of marijuana from the brown evidence bag. "Do you believe this?" He tightened his grip on the teen.

"Where'd ya get dat nasty stuff?" Betsy twisted Joseph's ear. "Ya know better dan ta get tangled up in stuff like dis." She fed Joseph a piece of her mind as he walked down the sidewalk to the waiting squad car.

When she came back inside, she burst into tears and wailed, "My baby, my baby boy…"

"Look what ya done." Thomas glared at the pastor and stormed into the church.

When the musicians played softly, Betsy's wails threatened to drown them out. Her children scooted to the end of the pew, wide-eyed, and silent for a change.

Finally, when it was time for the worship service to start, Miz Pennington had enough. She hobbled her way across the sanctuary, and paused in front of Betsy, frowning.

"That'll be enough of this caterwauling. This is God's house. Show some respect." She shook her cane at her then leaned in close. "Be strong, Betsy. It'll be okay."

Betsy hushed her sobbing.

"That's better." Miz Pennington gimped to her seat and sat down without pretense while a hush settled over the congregation.

Betsy got her hankey out, dried her eyes, then blew her nose so loudly that it could be heard on the back pew. Everyone burst out laughing. Betsy fumed and Miz Pennington frowned.

4 Show Them Love

That evening Betsy's phone rang. She didn't recognize the number. "Hello…"

"Mommm, Ya gotta get me outta here. Can't ya bail me out?"

"Well, ya shouldn't have done it. Ya know how nasty dat stuff is. Why'd ya do it?"

"Ya know why. Ya work hard and dere's never enuff money ta buy da food ev'rybody needs. If'n I sold baseball cards, mowed lawns, or did anythin' else, wud ya be dis upset with me? No. I don't think so. Sellin' da drugs was a fast way to buy da shoes dat da girls and Peter needed. Who'd ya think bought school supplies? I did.

I knew it was wrong ta do dat. I've been ta da DARE assemblies, read da pamphlets, and heard da speeches. It don't matter ta me one way or da other what dey did with da drugs. Who am I ta judge dem?"

"Dat's enough, Joseph. I do my best for ya kids."

"We cud have so much more if'n dad didn't drink away any money we do scrounge up. Who's gonna bring in da extra cash now dat I'm locked up? Hailey, maybe?"

Just then Betsy heard the guard in the background yell, "Freeman, your time is up. Let's go."

"Please, Mom…"

Dial tone!

When Betsy saw Joseph at his hearing the next morning, she sobbed loudly.

Bailiff Fox approached. "You need to simmer down, lady. Judge Brown does not like drama in the courtroom."

"You ain't seen nothin' yet. I can do it up all royal like if'n ya want."

Betsy's cries quieted to a sniffle. She looked across the room at the Johnsons. *Dere not bad people. Dey've been nice ta me and da family. Dey're livin' proof of love.*

I ain't never shown my kids da affection dey need. Could be why dere such awful brats cuz I'm mean, sharp-tongued, and bossy like my mama was. I don't know how ta fix dat.

She shivered as she remembered the beatings she'd endured. All these years later, her mama's angry words echoed in her ears. *"You are stupid, lazy, and a good-for-nothing idiot!" I sat dere with my homework spread out in front of me. I didn't get long division and parts of da speech. School was hard... If'n, I had somethin' good bout me dat my mama cared about; she would have been happier with me. She didn't know dat I snuck out ta Miz Pennington's ta let her cool down when dere was a fire in her belly.*

My Sunday School teacher would wrap her arms around me, dry my tears, and rock us back and forth on her porch swing. That's when I felt loved and happy inside. My mama's beatin's faded, and God felt real ta me. I wish dat Miz Pennington could've been my mama instead of her.

The judge entered the courtroom and brought Betsy's thoughts to an abrupt halt. She glanced over at her son bound in chains, flanked by two guard. His public defence attorney wore a cheap suit with perfume strong enough that the people in the next row coughed dramatically.

Guess I ain't da only one dat stinks up da pew.

She's a regular skunk cabbage. I don't trust her any further than I could throw her.

When she stood on Joseph's behalf, Betsy saw her slippery work at hand. "Your Honor, I would like to propose a plea deal with my client. It's his first charge, so maybe we can work something out."

"Councillors, Approach the bench." The judge motioned to them. "What's this all about?"

The lawyer grabbed the loose papers from her briefcase and handed the file to the judge. "Um, this is not the right file. This court admonishes you to be more professional. This is not the first time you disrespected the court with your lack of professionalism. Should it continue, I'll contact your superiors at the bar association."

"Sorry. Your Honor. I meant no disrespect to the court. I just got the case an hour ago and have not had sufficient time to organize the files."

"Will you need a continuance?"

"No, we can proceed. It looks cut and dried."

"As you will. Let's proceed to the Joseph Freeman case."

The courtroom grew tense as the attorney's talked on and on about what should happen to Joseph. Finally, Betsy watched as the councils returned to their places and the judge spoke again.

"Joseph Freeman, your attorney wants you to take a plea deal for a lesser sentence. Is that something that you want to do?"

"What's da catch?" Joseph shot back.

Betsy stood and looked directly at her son. "Ya need ta show some respect ta da judge and your attorney."

Joseph glared at his mother.

His attorney came back to the defendant's podium and explained the Joseph the terms of the plea deal.

"I ain't givin' up my contacts, so ya'll can pound salt." Joseph shook his hair from his eyes. "I reject da terms, and I ain't signin' nothin' ta say anythin' else." Joseph bellowed at the judge.

"It is very clear, young man, that you do not respect your mother, the law, or this courtroom. I might have been minded sending you to a rehabilitation or community support program, had I thought such a place would have benefitted you. However, your actions today suggest that you need a stronger remedy and I have decided that you need a year in Juvenile Corrections Facility in Boonville. You may say good-bye to your mother."

Joseph slowly made his way across the room. "Sorry Mom. I ain't tellin' nobody nothin', and don't ya neither." He narrowed his eyes threateningly.

"Rot in Juvie for all I care." She retorted then turned and rushed out the door overcome by emotions.

~

After Joseph's hearing, Pastor Johnson was in his study when Miz Pennington knocked on the door. "Come in, my dear, what brings you to my office?" Pastor Johnson led her to a comfortable chair. She situated herself then said, "Well, you see, Sonny, God told me to talk to you about the Freemans."

"You know them?" Pastor Johnson's jaw dropped open.

"Yeah, Betsy grew up in this here church. Her granddaddy's a foundin' member, but her mama never lived a righteous life. She became a slave to alcohol and hurt that little girl in drunken rages. Betsy often came to Sunday School with bruises. Believe you me, I wanted to take Bertha Fallon out behind the woodshed and give her a dose of what she gave her daughter, but hitting another person is still wrong."

"Poor girl. Why was her mother so mean to her?"

"She came about during a one-night stand, and she looks like her father who's a man she'd rather forget about. He met his demise in an accident at the lumber mill." *The pastor doesn't need the other sordid details.*

She cleared her throat and continued. "Betsy was an innocent child. Some would say that the meanness and bitterness caused the cancer that took Bertha's life. I don't have any idee if she made it to Heaven or not."

"You don't say." Pastor Johnson stretched and leaned back in his chair. He did not want this to be a gossip session, but he needed to learn how to help them.

"What about Mr. Freeman?"

"You mean Thomas? He was raised in these here parts. His daddy, the town drunkard, never held down a job. The story floating around these hills is that his mama, Caroline, done ran off with another man when Thomas was a wee lad. I wouldn't put trust in the rumor mill, especially when it comes to the Freeman clan.

"Thomas's granny and grandpappy raised him, but they up and died before his sixteenth birthday. He had no one who cared what he did or where he went."

"His daddy was a deadbeat parent. He never showed any love or respect for the boy. Then, one night another tragedy struck Thomas's life. His dad, Herbert Freeman Jr. was drunker than a skunk, and he drove right into a tree on Devil's Elbow just outside of town. That's how come Thomas inherited the farm.

"He got himself in a bit of trouble and did jail time. Part of his conditions when he got out was that he had to attend church. That's where he met Betsy. First thing ya' know those young'uns done ran off and got hitched."

"You don't say. Where do they live?"

"Over on Yorktown Road, just past Highway 721. It's run down now, but it was a nice piece of property back in the day."

Pastor Johnson stood. "Thank you for coming today." He helped her to her feet and handed her the cane to steady her feeble steps.

"Show them love, Pastor, that's all they need."

"Good advice, Miz Pennington."

"I'll be praying for you." She turned and headed down the steps and into the parking lot.

Pastor Johnson sat back down at his desk, and he

could not get the words of Miz Pennington out of his mind. "Show them love…"

How God? I don't know how to reach them.

That evening at supper, Pastor Johnson brought up his conversation about the Freeman family. "Miz Pennington's words still haunt me. Maybe we should go check out where they live, so we know how to help them. Vanessa, you, and Brianna hurry to get the dishes done. Boys, chores, now!" The children scattered and were done in a flash.

They ran to the van, jumped in, and headed across town to Highway 721. Pastor Johnson turned left onto Yorktown Road and found the farm sitting up on a hill.

When they pulled into the Freeman's driveway, Pastor Johnson thought, *The Freeman farm looks like a drunkard on a hill. The buildings have not seen a paintbrush in many years. The roof sagged as if it was soggy crêpe paper after a rainstorm. The house stood lopsided and crumbling apart. The grass is tall, waving in the wind.* Pastor Johnson expected to see the orange "Condemned" sign on the front door.

"Daddy, this place is yucky." Briana blurted.

"Yeah," said Jonathan. "They have a big barn that would be fun to play in."

"No way, buddy," piped up Evan, "Do you want to spend the rest of your life in a wheelchair?"

"Let's get out of here. This place creeps me out." Vanessa, his teenaged daughter, shivered.

Pastor Johnson put the van in reverse and headed back toward town. "Who wants ice cream?"

He tried to distract the children from what they saw.

"Me!" echoed loudly in his ears.

As they pulled up to the Dairy Shoppe, Pastor Johnson saw the Freemans at a picnic table fighting like a bunch of rabid dogs.

"Dis is not da first time you stole from us," screeched Betsy at the top of her lungs. "We should call da cops and send ya ta juvie just like your brother. Is dat what ya want?"

"How am I s'posed ta pay for my girl stuff?" Hailey shouted back.

"Ya work for it," Betsy yelled at her. "I started doin' odd jobs at twelve years of age, like babysittin', cleanin', and other stuff."

"How am I gonna do dat when I gotta watch dese brats while ya work?"

Betsy had nothing else to say. Hailey had a point.

~

That is when God spoke to Pastor Johnson.
Now. Love the Freemans.
But, God, I am out with my family.
Do you want to love your neighbor or not?
Yes, Father.
Then do what I am asking of you. Go to the Freemans.

Pastor Johnson walked across the parking lot. "Good evening, folks. Is there anything that I can do to help you?"

"Not dat it's any of your business, but we got a little thief here, now we ain't got da money ta pay for an ice cream cake for Jenny's birthday."

"Wait right here." Pastor Johnson went into Dairy Shoppe and bought their ice cream cake. It cost him thirty dollars, but he did what God asked him to do. You could have heard a pin drop as he walked back across the lot and laid a package on the table.

"Here you go. I had them cut it for you. In this bag is your silverware, napkins, and plates. Hope you enjoy it."

The Freemans stared at Pastor Johnson dumbfounded.

"Now why'd he go and do a thing like dat? Tryin' ta butter us up so we won't report him again?" Betsy wondered.

The kids ignored them and loaded their plates with cake. "Ya'll can fuss and fight all ya want, but we're celebratin'. If'n I was ya, I'd shut up and get some cake before it's gone." Peter interjected.

Betsy silently grabbed a fork and placed a large piece on her plate.

Thomas grumbled, "I don't like acceptin' charity, 'specially from da likes of da Johnsons. It always comes with strings attached."

"Oh, shut up, Thomas," Betsy shot back. "At least Jenny got a birthday cake this year."

~

Pastor Johnson went back inside, and ordered his family's treats, chocolate-covered ice cream cones with sprinkles.

"There's no way your family gets cones. We saw what you did. Why should you have to pay for something you didn't get to enjoy? How many are in your family?"

"Six, including my wife and I."

Within a few minutes, an array of ice cream sundaes and banana splits sat on the counter. "Okay, Pastor, here you go." The clerk put everything in a cardboard box.

When he reached for his wallets, the manager stepped forward. "Put that wallet back. This order is on the house." The workers applauded as he opened the door and headed to his van.

It pays to listen to You, Father. He thought.

5 I'll Call Da Police!

"Hailey, get in here, and do da dishes!" Betsy shouted from the kitchen. The sink and counters overflowed making the house smell like a dumpster on a hot summer's day. The odor made Betsy nauseous, and what's more, she was still angry about last night's birthday cake incident.

Not wanting to move from her spot on the threadbare couch, Hailey hollered back, "I'm busy."

"No, yer not. Get in here now!"

As quick as greased lightning, her dad yanked her off the couch and whaled the tar out of her. *Thwap! Thwap!* The belt stung like an attack of yellow jackets while she gagged at the odor of cheap beer and sweat. He breathed right into her face. "Ya heard yer mother. Get buithy."

"I hate you!" Hailey screamed at his back, then she limped off to the kitchen. After what seemed like hours of work, still seething, she thundered up the stairs and then flopped down on the bed. *"Ow!"* she groaned as she felt the soreness where the belt left its welts. *At least dere's no bleedin' dis time.* She rolled over and looked at the clock. "I'm late," Hailey angrily sputtered and sprayed a little cheap perfume on to cover up her odor.

If'n Dad wouldn't be such a lazy bum and fix da shower, I'd be able ta get cleaner. At least when I'm at school da gym teacher lets me shower privately, so I don't stink so much. Specially at certain times of da month. Glad for her kindness ta me.

She shrugged into her raggedy jacket and backpack, opened the window, shinnied down the tree, and raced in the shadows alongside the edge of the property. Hailey popped out from behind the shrubs and opened the door to a sports car waiting for her a hundred feet down the road.

"What took you so long? I thought you stood me up." Jeannie complained as she put the car into gear and squealed her tires.

"Had ta do da dishes," Hailey muttered, out of breath.

"Old man beat you again?" Jeannie took off like a rocket and then halted quickly at the stop sign.

"Yep."

"Sorry. Forget about him. Let's have a little fun." Jeannie skidded to a stop and shoved the gearshift into Park.

Hailey looked around the mall parking lot and smiled. After her dad's beating, she was ready for a diversion.

"Be careful, and don't let the cops stop you. Remember, go only for the wallets. No purses." Jeannie grabbed her oversized purse while Hailey clutched her backpack.

"Let's do dis." Hailey opened the car door and ran to the side entrance of the mall. She made her way inside cautiously looking around for any potential victims. *Dere's one! Got da wallet. Dat was easy.* She walked the aisles from store to store, gathering wallets and whatever she could get her sticky fingers on. Soon, Jeannie motioned to her from another store, and they ran as fast as they could toward separate exits. She almost made it out when a security officer stepped in front of her. "Excuse me, Miss, I need you to come with me."

"Why?" She turned and looked for her friend. *Figures. Da cops never catch Jeannie.*

At that moment, another guard came and joined his colleague.

"Going somewhere, little lady?"

Hailey said nothing.

"Ever hear of the long arm of the law?"

"No."

"Well, today's your lucky day because you just got to meet it."

Hailey screamed at them. "Ya let go of me right now!"

"Why would we do a thing like that?" One guard wrestled her arms behind her back while the other one clipped the cuffs on her. She screeched as the restraints rubbed her sore back.

Hailey wriggled, but the guards were always one step ahead of her. They took her into an empty room with a chair in the center of the floor. "Here we are. Now we wait."

"For what?"

"The police, of course."

"I ain't goin' nowhere with dem. I got rights."

"Think what you want, little lady. The police are

on their way." He opened the metal door and let it slam.

When Officer Wellington arrived, Hailey fought like a cornered tiger. *"Shoulda known it was another Freeman."* He thought.

Despite all her efforts, she still ended up at the police station. She furiously paced the holding cell, scowled, and punched the wall until her knuckles bled. "Not fair!" Hailey screamed at the top of her lungs. "I'm not a thief, t'was shoppin', dat's all."

"Wrong," interrupted Deputy Jones, "The videotape has proof. You and your little friend were pickpocketing a lot of people in the stores. We'll find the missing wallets when we search your backpack."

"Don't ya dare touch it. Dat's my stuff." Hailey gritted her teeth, shut her eyes tight, lowered her brows, and her mouth tightened in a straight line.

"No can do," Deputy Jones retorted.

Hailey flopped down on the hard bunk and winced, then curled into a ball spent from her tantrum. "It wasn't my fault," she mumbled and squeezed her eyes tightly shut. *Da girls and me need some new undies, t-shirts, and other stuff. How am I gonna get da things we need? Mom ain't gettin' it for us, so we gotta figure a way to get da things we need. It's kinda sad when yer own mother can't take care of ya.*

~

The door of the police station burst open, and Hailey's family arrived in their usual style, wild and loud. Betsy marched up to the desk and rudely yelled at the deputy through the protective glass vent. "Excuse me, you're holdin' my baby girl, Hailey, here and ya betta let her go at once or I'll…"

"What? Call the police?" The deputy chuckled. "Ma'am, in case you didn't notice, we are the police. We catch people who do things against the law. Your daughter was on a pickpocketing spree tonight, and that's a crime."

Betsy huffed. "Let me see her right now or else…"

"What? You'll call the police? We've already been over that."

Betsy glowered and drew in a deep breath.

Deputy Jones glared back at her. "If you don't shut your pie hole and behave, I'll throw your sorry carcass out of here."

She turned on her heels. *Flip! Flap!* Her ratty tennis shoes slapped the tile floors as she stomped off to the waiting area. If her face were any redder, she'd burst into flames.

~

The next morning, Betsy sat on the edge of her seat. Big tears slid silently down her cheeks as Hailey looked like a deer in the headlights. Her Public Defense Attorney stood silently as the judge read the charges of larceny of an amount over $1000 but under $3000. Turning to his officer of the court, he asked, "Bailiff Fox, can you tell me if the money was returned to the victims?"

"Yes. All wallets from Hailey's backpack had not been undisturbed."

"Thank you."

Judge Brown cleared his throat. "Hailey Freeman, there is mercy, which is a favor that a person doesn't deserve. Because of your first offense, and your family's situation, I am sentencing you to one hundred hours of community service and one year of probation.

You don't deserve the light sentence, but that is where mercy comes in. Do you understand?"

Hailey nodded.

However," the judge continued, "If you violate the probation, expect to find yourself in juvenile detention so fast that it will make your head spin. Got it?"

"Yes, Yer Honor." Hailey squeaked.

"Go now and behave yourself. Stay away from Jeannie, do your community service, and don't let me see you back in this court again." His gavel came down.

Hailey ran to her mom's side. I'm sorry. I was just tryin' ta get some money ta help us out. It scared me so bad last night. Da clankin' and bangin,' buzzin' of da doors echoed like a hollow cave. Da sounds still ring in my ears."

"Good. Ya heard da judge. Stay outta trouble."

"No worries. I'm done gettin' in trouble." Hailey sighed.

6 Through Mashed Potatoes and Gravy

The end of day school bell rang. Hailey Freeman made her way to her locker and grabbed her tattered jacket. She hoisted her backpack over her shoulder and pushed and shoved her way down the stairs and through the double doors.

Her mom's words this morning still scorched her ears. *Ya better be startin' da Community Service, or da judge is comin' after ya. Yer brother is gone away and I cain't have ya locked up too. Do what yer s'posed ta do.*

Who's gonna take care of da kids if I'm tied up? Hailey sighed as she walked down the street to the soup kitchen.

The door screeched open and slammed with a bang loud enough to wake the dead. Several volunteers stopped what they were doing as silence reigned for one golden moment.

Hailey Freeman trooped in like a marching band drummer and hung her threadbare coat on the rack. She stomped into the service area where her most-hated teacher, Mrs. Hudson, stood at the ancient stove.

"About time you showed up," she growled. "Where have you been?"

"Round," Hailey rolled her eyes.

"The judge wanted your community service to start last week. Do you know how much trouble I went through to keep you out of juvie? Especially since you missed a whole week of Community Service. Never mind. You are here now, and that's what counts."

Hailey scowled. The judge's booming voice echoed in her ears. *If you violate the probation, expect to find yourself in juvenile detention so fast that it will make your head spin.* She gritted her teeth and looked at the enormous pot steaming on the rickety old stove.

Witch's brew.

Mrs. Hudson glared at her. "Did you hear what I said, young lady?"

"No."

"You need to pay attention for once in your life. I told you before when you were wool-gathering that the first thing on your list of chores is to clean the bathrooms."

"What for?" she spat. "Dey're homeless bums. Dey're used ta a little dirt."

Mrs. Hudson bit her tongue to keep from saying. *And so are you, but a good cleaning won't hurt you anyway.*

"Hailey! That is quite enough. Now! Get busy." Mrs. Hudson roared.

She turned. *Nag. Nag, Nag.* Her knees high, feet heavily stomped, and frowned like an upside-down clown. Hailey stiffly marched toward the restrooms.

Cleaning bathrooms ranks up dere with goin' ta da dentist.

Hailey plugged her nose. *Dis place smells like an outhouse.* She sprayed everything down and gingerly with one hand wiped everything with the same sponge. The mirrors showed streaks where she shot them with the cleaner. The sink still had hairballs in them, and the toilets still had a ring around them. Water stood in puddles across the floor. She tossed the supplies into the closet and slammed the door shut. "Dere, all done, ya majesty."

"Are you ready for inspection?"

"Whadd'ya mean by dat?" Hailey raised her eyebrows.

While her teacher went to examine her work, Hailey nibbled nervously on her fingernails. *She won't notice.*

When Mrs. Hudson popped her head back out of

the bathroom, she growled. "A job half done is not done at all. You must do it again."

She noticed.

Hailey yanked the closet door open like a tornado ripping at hinges in a storm. She grabbed the cleaning supplies and haphazardly threw them into her bucket. *Crash! Bang! Slosh! Gurgle!* Bottles tumbled to the floor and leaked their contents together in a huge puddle. She whirled and stomped off toward the bathroom.

"Excuse me, young lady. When we make a mess, we clean it up. Didn't your mama ever teach you that?" Mrs. Hudson glared at her.

"Leave her out of dis!" Hailey grabbed the mop. *Slip! Slap!* It went on until the bubbly chemicals were all cleaned up. Then she clumped off toward the bathrooms to please 'her majesty'.

When she was through, Mrs. Hudson checked her work again. "Good job. I knew you could do it," and she patted her on the shoulder.

Hailey whirled. "Don't touch me!" Her bruises from last night's beating still hurt.

Mrs. Hudson pulled her hand back like she was singed with a hot iron. She sighed and looked heavenward. *No matter what I do, I can't break through to Hailey.*

~

At that moment, the door opened, and cool air swirled in the room as Deborah, Vanessa, and Brianna Johnson burst in loaded down with foodstuff.

"Don't just stand there, Hailey, help them bring in

the rest of the groceries." *Mrs. Hudson bellowed. Screaming seems to be the only language she knows.*

Hailey grabbed her coat, scowled, and silently obeyed.

"Thank you." Vanessa gave her a warm smile.

"By the looks of things, we are going to eat well tonight." Mrs. Hudson declared happily. "Where did you get all this food?"

"A generous donor," Deborah replied softly.

Hailey watched as Mrs. Hudson hugged the newcomer. *It's the same donor who supplied the classrooms and sends gift baskets to ones in need of encouragement.*

~

"Wish someone would do dat ta me. I cud use hugs If'n my dad didn't beat me so much." Hailey thought.

Hailey's stomach growled as she stepped up to the counter and worked alongside Vanessa. Neither girl spoke much as they washed and diced vegetables for salads.

Vanessa tried to engage her in small talk about school, but Hailey remained aloof.

I don't need ta talk ta her. Dis is community service. When my hours are in, I'll never come back ta dis creepy place.

It was not long before the doors opened, and several cheerful people entered. "Good afternoon, everybody."

Hailey hated upbeat people. They grated on her last nerve, especially when she was hungry. Her stomach had been growling since noon.

The crew loaded the large steaming pans onto the serving counter. Hailey had never seen this much food.

Soon, Mrs. Hudson called everyone into the kitchen. "Everything is ready to serve, but we will eat before the line forms outside the door." Mrs. Hudson and the volunteers removed the metal lids from the serving trays, and Deborah prayed a blessing over their food.

Hailey's mouth watered as the aromas rose from the pans and wafted past her nostrils. "Mmm," she sighed happily, grabbed a tray, and got in the back of the line. A smile crossed her face. *Finally, I can stop this tummy from growlin'.*

Vanessa waved to Hailey, "Come up here with me."

She's nice ta me. Da sooner I get my food, da happier I'll be. I guess it would be okay ta slip up da line.

"We get to pick what we serve," Vanessa blurted.

"I want mashed potatoes. Why don't you serve the gravy so, we can be together? I'll show you how to do it."

"Okay," Hailey agreed. *I don't wanna be friends, but I'm hungry.*

When they sat down at the table, she asked her, "Why'd dey pray for da food?"

"Because we thank God for providing everything for us." Vanessa patiently explained.

"God? Dat's weird. I thought we were da ones slavin' in da kitchen. How does He have anythin' ta do with a good meal?" Hailey shoved her mouth full of mashed potatoes and gravy. "Dis food's good," she said after she swallowed.

"Coming here isn't so bad, is it?" Vanessa smiled.

Hailey shook her head and stuffed the rest of her roll into her mouth.

Soon, it was time to serve. Faces peered through the steamy windows. People wiped the windows with scarves and mittens. "Hurry up! We're starved." They chanted. Hailey and Vanessa walked to the door and unlocked it when the clock struck five. Billows of people shoved their way through the doors.

"Where'd dey come from?" Hailey inquired as they walked back to the serving table.

"Some are homeless; others have lost jobs and can't afford to feed their families; and several are lonely and elderly who enjoy the company in the evenings," Vanessa replied.

"How do ya know?"

"Easy. By listening to them talk. They'll tell you

their problems, and it makes them feel better even if you can't solve their difficulties."

Hailey nodded but did not have time to say anything.

For the next two hours, all Hailey could focus on was the splat of the mashed potatoes, then she would plunk her ladle into the middle of the mound and dump her load of gravy in the tater well. They worked a pattern, *Splat! Plunk! Slosh!*

When one of the volunteers replaced the gravy pan, she looked down the line at the people waiting for food and saw a familiar face.

What was Kaitlyn Smith, the popular cheerleader doin' here, and who's dat with her? Dose kinds of people don't come ta soup kitchens like dis.

After the pan was in place, she resumed the pattern with Vanessa.

Kaitlyn won't notice me.

The next thing she knew, the popular girl stood in front of her.

"Hi! Don't you go to my school?"

Hailey glared at the girl. "Yeah. So. Is dere a problem with that? If'n so, we can settle it outside."

"Hailey, be nice," Vanessa advised. "We don't want to be fighting when we are serving others."

When the line of people ended, Hailey hesitantly asked Mrs. Hudson if she could make up some carry-out trays for her siblings.

"Are they hungry tonight?"

"Yes, and dey're home alone with my dad, and he never does anything ta feed dem while he's home." Hailey whirled with tears in her eyes.

Mrs. Hudson spoke softly to the girl. "You have

done a wonderful job tonight, thank you. Now, let's get those trays filled up."

She grabbed a big box and stuffed it to the brim. "Here you go Hailey. I'll see you tomorrow."

Hailey grabbed her coat, the big box, and walked through the door as Mrs. Hudson locked it behind her.

~

Deborah had pulled around the block and parked out of sight. When they spotted her, Vanessa opened the van door and stepped into the street. "Hailey, Mom will take you home tonight."

She hesitated, "I can walk."

"It's dark, and something bad could happen to you." Vanessa came back. "Hop in."

Hailey reluctantly gave in. "It'll be okay. This box is heavy and It's a long walk. I need ta get home as soon as I can." *Hope da kids are okay. I can't be with dem all da time.*

When they pulled onto Hailey's road, the van glided silently to a stop. Vanessa jumped out and handed the food box to her. Tears glistened in Hailey's eyes as she slipped through the hedges and disappeared into the darkness.

Da Johnsons are so nice ta our family.

~

When Hailey opened the rickety kitchen door, her drunken dad met her.

"Where ya been? Isn't it yer job ta take care of dese brats?" Thomas slurred his words. "And where's thuppa?"

"Here." Hailey pushed a tray across the cluttered table.

"Where ya swipe dis?" He garbled.

"Didn't steal," Hailey shouted back at him. "Remember, I got community service. Gotta do it or go ta juvie like Joseph. Den who'd take care of yer kids?" She turned her face away from his rotten-smelling breath. *Thwap!* The belt stung her shoulders and back.

"Don't thath me!" When he'd finished beating her, he staggered to the table, opened a tray, and wolfed down the contents.

When he tottered off to the bedroom, Hailey called her siblings from their hiding places. "Here ya go. Ya better eat and get ta bed."

They sat on the threadbare couch, then gobbled down the food like there was no tomorrow.

After they ate, Hailey put the leftover milk in the fridge, gathered the trash, and plopped it in the cans at the corner of the house. She saw the lights of the family car coming up the driveway as she headed back inside. She was happy that her mom would have something decent to eat tonight.

Mom seemed glad! Hailey sighed as she ascended the stairs. *Da folks at da soup kitchen were okay. Dis Community Service means dinner on da table every night. I like havin' a full tummy at bedtime. Da growlin' stomach keeps my eyelids open.*

7 I Did My Homework

Hailey climbed the stairs to her room, shoved the window up, and breathed deeply of the cool night air. *Ahhh!* She lifted her eyes to the dark sky. The pale crescent moon shone like a silvery claw in the night sky and the blanket of stars stretched to infinity. *God, um, thanks for dinner for ev'rybody. But I gotta ask ya. Can ya make dad quit beatin' us up?*

The only sound was the distant barking of their neighbor's dog. Hailey felt peaceful at that moment. She shivered a little, then closed the window, sat down at her rickety old desk, and pulled out her homework. Hailey never did her school assignments, but tonight was different. Her tummy was full, and she felt happy because Mama smiled at her.

She gingerly opened her math book and stared at the page as if it held the deep secrets of the world. *There's gotta be a key somewhere ta unlock dat terrible word, algebra!* After peering into the blackened pools on the page, she found the key on the sidebar, and suddenly, the light came on in her mind, and the rest of the problems were a piece of cake.

Within an hour, Hailey finished her last homework problem. She yawned, and climbed between the cold sheets, shivered, curled into a ball, and fell asleep with a hope of better days ahead.

Then into her dreams came blood-curdling screams. She jarred awake and bolted upright in her bed. Her heartbeat thumped in her ears. *There it was again. Somethin's not right.*

Hailey threw on her threadbare robe, thundered down the stairs, and raced into the kitchen.

Hailey yelled, "Oh, no you don't! You're not gonna get by with hittin' her again!"

Dad's fist connected with her mom's face.

Thud! Betsy hit the floor. Blood gushed from her nose and ran down her chin. Her eyes swelled and turned a sickly shade of purple.

Somebody's gotta end dis now before he kills her!

Peter raced downstairs at that moment. Within a split second, he grabbed his mom's arm, and dragged her behind the livingroom couch. His dad stood there wildly swinging in the air, not aware that his target was gone.

Betsy started moaning in pain. She tried to string her thoughts together, but her shock wouldn't let her.

~

Hailey shoved her dad backward. She screamed at him, "What do ya think you're doin', ya big bully? Dat's my mom ya beat up. Da same one who works like a slave ta keep da wolf from da door. What do ya gotta say for your sorry self?"

Thomas glared at her through bloodshot eyes. "Don't ya thath me, or ya get da same medicine."

Hailey stared right back at him. "Ya ever lay a hand on her again; I'll call da cops. Ya got dat?"

"Alright, Hailey I never thought ya had it in ya ta be so sassy ta yer dad. Yer gonna pay for it."

"Ooh, I'm scared. What's da worst ya can do ta me? Pull out yer belt again?"

Thomas flailed at her, but Hailey ducked and stepped aside. When she spun to leave the room, he grabbed Joseph's baseball bat, and hit her on the back of the head. Hailey crumpled to the floor. All went black.

~

Angrily, Peter yanked the bat out of his dad's hands. "Now look what ya did. You oughtta rot in jail for dis. Go ta bed before somebody else gets hurt." Peter spun him around and roughly marched him to the downstairs bedroom. "Don't ya dare come out of dere before daylight." Peter stood and watched the bedroom door.

~

By sheer force of her will, Betsy drug her body to the couch and pulled herself up. *I gotta think of my kids more dan me.* She turned her head gingerly to look at Hailey still out cold from her injuries. *Brave, brave Hailey. She took a hit for me.*

Betsy stumbled to the freezer and grabbed a bag of peas. She thumped it a couple timed on the counter, then wrapped it in a little towel. Still seeing stars, but determined to take care of her girl, she pushed through the fog.

Hailey roused when her mom put the pack on the back of her head. "Ya okay?" Betsy held her daughter's hand. A solitary tear trickled down her bruised cheek.

"It's like I've been on a merry-go-round dat won't let me off. I wanna throw up."

Determined, she pulled out her phone and dialed 911. As it rang, she stroked her daughter's hand. "It'll be okay."

The sirens cut through the silence of the night. Help was on its way.

I know dis is gonna wake ev'rybody up, but they need to dress quickly to go with us.

"Take a deep breath." The paramedic encouraged Betsy. "Lay back on the gurney and let us do our work."

"What bout Hailey? She should go first."

"Don't worry about her. We have a second crew on the way. Was anyone else injured?"

"No."

Officer Wellington leaned over the gurney. "The only way this cycle is going to stop is for you to press charges. Are you willing to do that for the sake of your kids?"

"Even though I don't want to, I have ta say yes. He hits on me all da time. I don't like it, but when my kids get hurt, dat's where I draw da line."

"Okey-dokey, just sign here and it's done."

When they arrived by ambulance at the hospital, Betsy watched the doctors and nurses swarm around Hailey like yellowjackets around a slab of meat. Her world slowly began to swirl and tighten into a narrow tunnel. She powered through the darkness as bravely as she could for her daughter, willing herself to be there in the moment. One of the attending physicians gently placed some kind of collar around Hailey's neck. Little red lights shone in Betsy's vision. They flashed like the blinkers at Main and 14th. *Off. On. Off. On.* The darkness slowly enveloped her. Despite her best efforts, Betsy gave way to oblivion.

She awoke as the staff moved her from the gurney onto a hospital bed. Betsy could barely open her eyes, and her ribs throbbed intensely.

She angrily brushed her hair out of her face. When Doctor Bender entered the cubicle, Betsy blurted, "How's Hailey doin' over dere?"

"She is resting now, but she mentioned other children. Where are they?"

"Some nice lady took dem for 'mergent care."

Betsy shakily drew in a deep breath and gasped as Dr. Bender began his exam.

"Did your husband do this?" The doctor tried to keep his voice from betraying the anger he felt. "Betsy, you are bruised from head to toe. There are injuries that look a little older than the fresh marks. The law says that I must report the abuse to the authorities."

"I already talked ta da big police dude."

"Officer Wellington?"

"Sounds right." Betsy winced when the doctor probed another spot.

"This time your husband is on thin ice. Nobody has a right to batter you and your daughter like this. I'm going to step out of the room now. He paged the on-call social worker. "It's gonna be a loooong night!" He glanced at the charge nurse staring at the computer screen.

"Yep," She clacked the keys like her life depended on it.

He popped his head back inside Betsy's curtain. "Do you have any friends to be with you? It's possible that we'll need to do emergency surgery, so you may want someone to be with you since your husband won't be able to be here." Dr. Bender wrote in a chart.

~

"Mama," Hailey called across the curtain, "Can ya ask Vanessa to go to my room and get my backpack? I'm gonna need some stuff out of it."

"Yeah, I'll call her for you." Betsy dialed Deborah's number.

"Sorry ta wake ya up, Mrs. Johnson. I need ya and Vanessa ta go ta da house. Hailey needs her backpack from her room, which is upstairs, and da last room on da right.

"Hailey and me got roughed up by you know who. We're both bad off..." Betsy sobbed, but it made her swollen eyes hurt. She hung up her phone and laid her head back on the pillow.

"A friend's comin'," Betsy informed the nurse.

"Good."

~

Deborah Johnson soon pulled back the curtain of Betsy's cubicle. She laid a hand gently on hers, and Betsy opened her eyes a little bit.

"Oh, dear girl. You weren't kidding! So sorry this happened." She pulled up a chair close to the bed. "Is there anything I can do for you?"

"Cud ya get me some ice chips? I'm not allowed anythin' ta eat or drink cuz dey're talkin' about me needin' surgery. Dat's why I called ya. I'm scared outta my mind."

Deborah walked over to Betsy's side table and

spooned a few chips from the Styrofoam cup.

"Here you go." Betsy opened her mouth and shoveled the chips in.

"Would you like me to pray for you and Hailey?"

"Yeah. Dat wud be nice."

Deborah's soft voice comforted Betsy, and she fell asleep knowing somehow that God cared for her.

~

Hailey Freeman awoke, confused, and agitated, thrashing around in her bed.

"Shhh." The nurse soothed her and injected more medicine in her IV.

"Why?" Hailey's fuzzy brain didn't register. Things were all vague and her headache raced to the top of the charts. She laid back on the pillows and breathed deeply.

Soon, Dr. Bender came back into Hailey's cubicle. "You know, if the bat would have hit one millimeter lower, you'd never walk again. We can repair the vertebrae after the swelling goes down.

"You have a serious concussion to go along with the vertebrae injury. That is why you are dizzy and nauseated. I'll give you some medicine to help with that, but you must stay as still as possible.

Do you remember what happened?"

"Kinda." *Thank God, Mom's gonna be okay. Dad woulda killed her for sure. If'n it weren't for Peter and me, one of us could've been pushin' up daisies.*

Hailey lowered her eyebrows, squeezed her eyes shut, wrinkled her nose, and shook like a leaf in a thunderstorm. She could feel the tears forming in the corner of her eyes, threatening to spill down her cheeks, but she willed them to stay put. *Cryin's for babies, and I'm a Freeman…*

~

Just then, Vanessa Johnson walked in with her backpack. She opened it for Hailey and removed the homework. "I'll take this to Mrs. Hudson as soon as I get to school, then I'll pick up your homework for you every day."

"Don't have ta do dat. Mrs. Hudson could have a heart 'tack."

They both smiled. *Vanessa could be a good friend.*

~

Vanessa looked back over her shoulder when she left Hailey's side. *Oh, dear God, Hailey's a pitiful sight with IV tubes everywhere and her neck in a brace. I don't know how my dad does this. Hospitals are scary places, and Hailey looks so small and alone on that gurney. Her face is bruised and swollen, and her lips are twice the size they should be. She must have face planted. How can I make it better for her?*

You can pray.

True.

The best thing you can do for Hailey is to be her friend regardless of how she acts.

~

Later that night as Deborah and Vanessa sat in the surgical waiting room when Betsy went to the operating room. She was bleeding internally, and needed emergency surgery to remove her lacerated spleen, and to repair broken bones. Betsy fell asleep with Hailey on her mind. Prayers surrounding her and the medical staff.

8 Dear Mama

Sunlight penetrated the tiny, barred window high up on the dark gray wall of Joseph Freeman's cell. Little sunbeams danced like miniature ballet dancers chasing the shadows away. He awoke from his dreamland, stood up, stretched, then bent to make his bed. The guard's words stuck in his head. *If a quarter won't bounce on the bed, ya gotta drop and do ten pushups, then make it right.*

I'm sure da guard had been in da army. Ev'rybody else thinks so too.

For the first time in his life Joseph had structure. He relished it because it helped him to focus. At home, he used to do whatever he wanted whenever he chose to do it. Here, he had to follow rules or there would be consequences... like having to scrub nasty toilets.

Joseph sat at the desk, trying to think of what to say in his weekly letter to his mama. That was his English assignment for the day.

Dear Mama: Hi. Hope you're doin' okay. I'm fine, so ya can stop worryin' about me. A few days ago, I hit rock bottom, and I called Pastor J. It seems dat da coppers have found new evidence dat could have me locked up til I'm 21. Dey may be bluffin', but it made me mad. Here I am behind bars, and I can't do nothin' ta help ya or myself.

Den Pastor J came and sat down with me and let me talk out my feelin's. He didn't try ta fix da problems himself but asked me what I thought I should do.

I told him I didn't know. Dat's why I called him. I yelled at him and da guards told me if I didn't settle down, I'd end up in lockdown for the rest of da day.

I said, "Sorry" and da guard growled back. "Ya better be." Dat guy scares me ta death.

After da guard left, Pastor J said, "You got a choice; be better or bitter." He said I can learn from my mistakes and move on to be a better man. Can ya believe dat? He called me a man, and I'm only fifteen!

I told him about Dad's drinkin' and beatin's. I worry about who's lookin' out for da kids while I'm away. Are dey getting' enuff food? Things gotta be bad for dem.

Pastor J told me that I can get through dis tough time, but I need ta make better choices. Above everythin', he told me dat I needed ta learn ta talk ta Jesus. Yeah right. I ain't about ta be shoutin' Hallelujah dis and Praise da Lord dat and still be doin' time here in juvie. He gave me lots ta think about.

My days are busy. We have school in da mornin' and in da afternoons; we go outside in da courtyard ta play sports if it's not rainin'. Volleyball is da best! I can make a lot of points off my serves.

Thursdays are Visitors' Day. Then, after supper we gotta do homework til lights out at 10 p.m. My grades are better dan da other school I was in. Da teachers here sit down with us and splain everythin' as we go along. You'll see a copy of my report card with dis letter. I can see ya in my mind's eye smilin' and dancin' around cuz juvie has changed me. I'm takin' things more seriously. Pastor J comes ta see me every week. Why don't you? He brought me some of my fave candy bars. Turns out he likes dem too.

We talk about lots of things. When da social worker told me about what happened ta you and Hailey, I was in a sour mood all week. I don't know if I can forgive Dad for what he did to ya both. It ain't fair!

Pastor J told me dat I need ta forgive him. It brought back so many memories of how he beat me too and Dad needs ta pay for what he done. Pastor J said dat da courts will see to it dat Dad gets what he deserves. But dere's somethin' else, God already judged him. It ain't up ta me ta be angry about somethin' dat has nothin' ta do with me. Dat ain't my job.

Den Pastor J said dat God took all da terrible things away when He hung dere on da cross. All I had ta do was ask Jesus ta forgive my wrong stuff and let Him worry about Dad's.

I can't forgive by myself, but dat's where God comes in. He forgave my mess ups, and He can do da same for Dad too. I feel so much happier dan I did before. Da anger toward Dad is gone. I hope ya both get better soon. I talk to Jesus everyday bout ya.

Your boy, Joseph

~

With Joseph's letter inside his suit coat pocket, Pastor Johnson glanced at his car's clock when he left the Juvenile Detention Center. An hour and a half later, he skidded to a stop, locked his car, raced up the steps, and rushed into the courtroom, scarcely in time. *From one Freeman to another.* Pastor Johnson panted quietly as the official walked to the front of the room.

Pastor Johnson saw on the big screen on the side of the wall, Betsy sitting up in a hospital bed with a well-dressed woman at her side.

Must be her attorney, Pastor Johnson thought.

He stood as Bailiff Willard Simpson called from his position at the judge's bench. "All rise for the Honorable Judge Henry Paxton. Your Honor, this is the case of The State vs. Mr. Thomas Freeman." He handed the thick folder to the justice, walked across the room, and stood at attention.

Pastor Johnson bowed his head and prayed as the judge harshly spoke to Thomas.

God, this man is at a crossroads with a lot of charges hanging over his head. He needs a Come to Jesus moment. Listen to all this, dear Lord. Five counts of child abuse, attempted murder, aggravated assault. He deserves what the judge is telling him, but could you have mercy on his soul, and help him to make the right decision about the Freemans' future?

Look at him, God. His shoulders are slumped, he's unshaven, with worn out tennis shoes; and I can smell his body odor way over here.

Did I not tell you to love the Freemans? Don't be quick to criticize him. He needs someone to show him a better way.

I have a feeling that You are talking about me.

Ding! Ding! Ding! Give the man a treat!

Hear that, God? He just pleaded not guilty. You know very well that he's not an innocent man. He got caught this time, but how many times has Thomas abused his wife and children about which you don't know?

Ut OH! Judge Paxton doesn't seem impressed. Things aren't going too well for Thomas, Oh Lord.

I know. Trust Me. I have a plan for him.

Do you do? I don't understand.

Even the worst among them can come to Me and find rest for their weary souls. That's what My grace is all about.

Pastor Johnson saw tears streaming down Betsy's eyes as she watched the proceedings.

Look at how much Thomas has hurt her, Father.

I know. She is beginning to turn her heart toward Me in her deepest pain. I will bring beauty from the ashes of her life.

Pastor Johnson watched as Judge Paxton turned to Prosecuting Attorney Michael Haynes. "What does The State recommend in this case?"

He stood and greeted Judge Paxton, then turned to Thomas, who stared out the window. "Excuse me, Mr. Freeman, I am talking to you."

God, look at Thomas. He can't see straight through his bleary eyes. How is that going to help Your plan?

Just wait and My answer will come to all your questions.

~

Thomas startled and blinked his eyes to clear his vision. "I heared ya."

"We're recommending twenty years to life in the state penitentiary for all counts. Mr. Freeman's record shows blatant, habitual disregard for others."

~

Father: Betsy's sobbing into her hands. It breaks my heart to see her in such a vulnerable position, but the brokenness hurts me too. As her spiritual shepherd, will You show me how to minister to her. Pastor Johnson wiped a tear from his eyes.

Thomas stood like a wooden statue. *Twenty years*

is stupid just cuz I wanna drink.

Prosecuting Attorney Haynes continued. "The State will consider a lesser sentence if Mr. Freeman checks himself into a detox hospital, gets a job, and attends AA regularly afterward." He nodded toward the judge and sat down.

Yeah right. I'm gonna rot ta death behind bars. Dat'll serve Betsy right. Thomas shifted his weight to his other foot.

Then, the Public Defense Attorney, Charles Browning, stood. "Folks, Mr. Freeman has had a hard life because he didn't have a mama around to take care of him…"

~

Pastor Johnson thought. *Oh, Boo Hoo! I've heard this routine a million times before. You can't paint a man as a saint when he's living like an abject sinner."*

Maybe not, but I can change a sinner into a saint.
True.

After a brief court recess, Judge Paxton spoke directly to Thomas. "You are making life difficult for yourself, Mr. Freeman. Besides all the outstanding charges, here is a copy of a twelve-month 'No Contact Order' that your wife filed yesterday. An action which is entirely justified if not significantly overdue. That means Betsy ran out of patience, waiting for you to mend your ways."

Thomas squirmed and looked away.

The judge continued. "Thomas Freeman, you have come to a crossroads. One way leads to twenty years to life in the state penitentiary, and the other one leads to the Sober Living Program. Then, Brocks Home to make a better man of yourself if you follow its rigorous intervention.

You have wasted your life on alcohol and ruined your marriage and family. The children are following in your footsteps.

If we have a trial, you will go to prison. This is your only chance for any kind of mercy from this court. Choose your future carefully, Mr. Freeman."

Thomas hung his head. *Intervention or prison? Da drink takes away da pain in my life.*

Without regard for his wife or children, he declared. "Yer Honor, I've been drinkin' a long time. It's in my blood. Not sure detox is gonna work."

~

Betsy disappeared from the screen.
Oh God, I hope she's okay. Pastor Johnson prayed.

~

Judge Paxton angrily grabbed his gavel and pounded it heavily on the bench. "You are despicable!"

Turning to the guards, Judge Paxton took a deep breath. "Take him away. I recommend three days of solitary confinement for him to think about his life choices. When Mr. Freeman comes back next month for the sentencing hearing, I'll need his answer."

Within seconds, they led Thomas from the courtroom.

~

Oh, dear God, help Thomas to make the right decision. Pastor Johnson prayed as he stood and walked out of the courtroom.

Next on my list is to visit Betsy and Hailey. He dialed his wife's number. "Hey Sweetheart, can you be ready to go with me to the hospital for a visitation? We need to check on Mrs. Freeman and her daughter."

"Yeah. Give me five minutes to freshen up." She wiped her hands on her kitchen towel.

When they arrived at the hospital, the minister reached into his suit coat pocket. "Here's a letter from Joseph."

"Really? Thanks." Betsy pulled the sheet up over her shoulders.

"How's my boy doin'? I miss him. Wish he could've been her to protect Hailey and me. We are both in a world of hurtin'."

"Joseph is doing as well as can. I'm sure you'll learn more in his letter." Sensing Betsy's restlessness, Pastor Johnson prayed. "Dear Father, You see the situation that the Freeman family are in. Please help Betsy and Hailey to heal quickly. And be with Thomas as he sits in his jail cell. He has a huge decision to make. Lead him out of his alcoholism and into freedom in You, Amen."

"Thank ya for prayin'." Betsy anxiously played with Joseph's letter in her hands.

~

Shortly after the Johnsons left, Hailey asked her mother to read the letter to her. "Ya gonna write back?"

"Yeah. When I get better, I wanna go ta see him."

"Me too, but I'm too young."

"Ya can write ta him."

Hailey said nothing because she had drifted off to sleep.

Betsy grabbed the pencil beside her bed and pulled a tablet from her purse.

Dear Joseph: Thank ya for yer letter. Da Preacher man gave it ta me. I'm happy ta hear from ya. It means a lot. Ya make me so proud. Ya done wrong, but good 's comin' from it.

T'was a scary time when your dad went haywire on dat night. He 's sittin' in a jail cell waitin' for his sentencin' next month. I watched his time in front of da judge. He weren't too happy with Dad. I ain't never seen da judge so mad.

Ya talked about forgiveness in yer letter. I know I need to do dat too. I just ain't ready yet. Dere's lots of things dat I gotta think bout first.

Dere's a difference 'tween da people dat do da Hallelujah thing, and da people dat really show others who dis Jesus man is. Da preacher man shows people love from his heart. Da other ones just say da words ta make dem selves look religious. I've been ta churches dat do dat. Dere religion stinks cuz dey don't help dose in need. Your Pap Fallon sure talked good on Sunday, but he was mean as a snake every other day of the week. Just sayin'.

Hailey and me are still in da hospital. I had surgery ta stop da bleedin' inside me. Got some broken ribs dat are sore, but doctors think I should be outta here early next week. Hailey will be here a while. She cud been paralyzed. Mama

9 Oh, Bother!

That night, Hailey struggled to sleep. Pain, both physically and emotionally, yapped like two little dogs at her heels. She tried hard to shove her anger away, but it kept coming back like a bad penny. She shifted uncomfortably around in her bed which awoke her mama. Betsy limped to her side and sat gingerly on the side of her bed. "What's wrong, girl? Why can't ya sleep? Can ya tell your mama what's goin' on?"

"When ya read Joseph's letter ta me, it made me think bout da forgiveness thing. What Dad done ta me can't be forgiven! He oughtta rot in a jail cell for da rest of his life. I don't care if'n he dies a horrible death cuz he beats us up all da time. I hate him!"

"I don't think hate's da right word, Hailey. Dat's what bad people do. Den dey turn out ta be criminals and get put away behind bars cuz hate leads to crime. Ya don't want dat, do ya?"

"No, but he should get a taste of his own medicine and see how he likes it. One good wallop and he's goners. Curtains. It'll be justice ta see dat happen."

"Don't wish bad on him yet. Maybe dis year away

will help him ta do better."

Hailey continued, "What good man hits his wife and kids? Good people don't hurt each other.

"Vanessa said dat I should forgive him. I'm a million miles away from doin' dat. Look, if ya hurt people, ya don't deserve forgiveness. Plain and simple. I know dat da Bible said to let go of da bad things dat happen, but I just can't do it." Hailey sighed, spent from her talk. She felt better and laid back on her pillow.

"Just close yer eyes and go ta sleep. If ya need anythin', I'll bring dem in with my whistle." Betsy patted her hand and limped off to her own bed.

Please don't.

~

"Good morning, Miss Hailey, Miz Betsy. It's a beautiful day, isn't it?" The nurse greeted them and opened the blinds. Brilliant sunlight flooded the room.

"Sunshine makes me happpppy..." Betsy started singing at the top of her lungs.

Must be the pain meds, the nurse thought. *Good stuff!*

~

"Aw, shut up, Mama," Hailey groaned. *Mama's singin' voice grates on my nerves without a concussion, but now it sounds like an old yeller hound under da porch yowlin' at da moon.* She hit the button on the pain pump.

Betsy awoke mid-morning, and she was angrier than a bear coming out of hibernation because several microphones dangled over her head. "Who let ya bozos in?"

"We're from Channel 6 News and we want an

exclusive interview about your situation. The community always resonates with human interest stories."

"Oh, so that's it. I'm a story, am I? Let me tell ya'll somethin' loud and clear, so yer feeble minds can understand. We ain't talkin' ta nobody about nothin'. Now shoo!"

"Your story could encourage other women to stand up and do the right thing to stop domestic abuse." The reporter begged. "Pleeease."

Betsy glared at them for a long silent moment. She was reading them like a book.

Okay, two could play this game. I can use dis circus ta help me and da kids. She huffed. "Lower yer voices. If'n ya wake Hailey up, yer gonna rue da day ya done waltzed in here like a bunch of clowns. Da long and short of it is dat we lost everythin'. Da county idiots busted into our house and got it in dere heads dat me and da kids don't have a house anymore. Dey condemned it. Dat means da kids and me got nothin'. No house, no clothes, NOTHIN' thanks ta da bunch of do-gooders. Now, git. I'm a sick woman and I'm done talkin'."

They faded like a cloud on the horizon.

"Thanks, Mom," Hailey whispered,"Dat's tellin' dem.

~

Clippety Clop! High heels clomped down the shiny waxed hallway toward Hailey's room. The sequined purple shoes stopped right beside Hailey's bed.

Now what? Betsy thought. *Don't dese people ever quit?*

"What do ya reckon yer doin' clumpin' down da

hall and bargin' into my room? Come over here so I can see yer ugly mug." Hailey shouted.

Go, Hailey, go! Betsy thought.

Screech! The chair moved across the highly waxed tile. Hailey's headache scale went off the charts, and she pushed the button on the pain pump.

"Hello. I'm Felicity Wells with Children's Social Services." She stuck her hand out to shake with Hailey, but she ignored it.

"What do ya think yer doin' here?" Betsy yelled at the intruder.

"The hospital social worker sent me to discuss Hailey's living arrangements when she gets out of the hospital."

"Whoa! Hold yer horses. Why can't I go home with my mama?" Hailey exploded.

"Because you must remain in the care of The State until things change with your housing situation or unless you have a living relative that she can live with."

"Nobody's goin' anywhere without my say-so. Ya'll are da ones who snuck into my house while we were laid up in da hospital. We were fine until ya put yer nose where it didn't belong. Now yer wantin' ta say dat Hailey cain't be with me. NO! I'll fight ya all da way ta da White House if'n I need to. My kids belong ta me. Ain't nobody walkin' off with dem. " Betsy threatened.

Unfazed, Felicity continued. "You don't have to give permission. Your children's case file arrived on my desk and it's my duty to investigate and place the children in foster homes. We want to make sure that the kids are safe."

"How dare ya people!" Hailey shouted angrily.

Hearing raised voices, the nurse ran into the room and swiftly yanked the reins of the conversation to a sudden stop, like bringing a racehorse to a halt at the finish line. "Excuse me, lady, we're done here. You must leave. Now! Hailey has sustained a severe injury and needs to be still and quiet."

Felicity closed her laptop bag. "I'm sorry. I'll come back when Hailey is feeling better." Her clomping high heels tapped out a rat-a-tat rhythm down the hall.

Hailey breathed deeply and exhaled slowly through her pursed lips. The numbers on the monitor came into a smooth rhythm as she relaxed.

"That's a girl. Just rest now. I'll put a 'Do Not Disturb' sign on your door." The nurse left the room, and they fell asleep until lunchtime.

~

That evening, Vanessa Johnson, and Mrs. Hudson visited Hailey.

"Hi!" she greeted them. Is somethin' wrong?"

"No, Hailey. I came to show you this." She handed her the homework sheet with a big red 100% at the top.

Hailey beamed from ear to ear.

"You've overcome so much, Hailey, and I'm so proud of you. I'll send your schoolwork with Vanessa, so you don't get behind. If you need any help, call me." She handed her a piece of paper with her number in bold letters.

"My soup kitchen duties await. I'm going to miss my mashed potato and gravy servers." She turned and waved goodbye to the girls.

Vanessa and Hailey looked at each other and burst out laughing.

"Remember what we said?" Hailey prompted.

"Yeah." Vanessa answered. "You said Mrs. Hudson would have a heart attack when she saw your homework."

"Yep, did ya see dat big ole fat 100% in red? I need ta frame dis."

"Let's try for another one." Vanessa opened the book and helped Hailey earn her next passing grade.

Then the conversation turned serious as Hailey told her about Felicity's visit. "I'm scared. Don't wanna go to foster care. What if they split us all up and I never see my siblings again?"

"You could stay with me. That would be fun, wouldn't it? I'll talk to my mom about it and let you know. I'll come back tomorrow, and we'll talk again." Vanessa stood and gathered her books and shoved them into her backpack.

"Let me know so Miss High Clickin' Heels can just walk on by." Hailey waved to Vanessa. *She's comin' ta be a good friend.*

~

Several days later, Betsy left the hospital. Since she couldn't go back to her own home, she found herself in a women's haven, recovering from her emergency surgery. The shelter's list of rules scared her spitless. *I can't do anythin' ta get thrown out on my ear by da people in charge of dis place. Dey say dat dey have mercy but I ain't seen it and I'm scared to find out if dey mean what dey said in da papers.*

With nothing stronger than over-the-counter pain relief allowed, Betsy curled up in a ball and stuffed her pillow in her mouth. She whimpered like a little puppy until another woman approached her bed.

"Ya may think you're all that and a bag of chips cuz you've been on TV, but I'm gonna kick ya to the moon if ya don't shut up."

Betsy opened her mouth with a nasty retort; gave

the woman a good old-fashioned stare down, and then for the first time in her life, she shut her yap and turned away.

The pain from her injuries was nothing compared to the agony she felt from losing her children. She wanted nothing more than to yell and scream, or kick something or hurt someone, but the rules said that Betsy could end up homeless if she took part in any violence.

When it came time for the daily group counseling, Betsy locked down tighter than Fort Knox. *My world may be spinnin' like a planet out of orbit, but all dese weepy li'l women don't need ta know dat. I can handle myself without splainin' my 'motions. I pack it all down tight inside until dere's no more room, den I explode, and it's all over. Talkin' about feelin's is a waste of time cuz I need a miracle, or I'll be beggin' in da streets with no hope of gettin' da kids back. Dat's far more important.*

~

After lunch, Deborah arrived with fresh clothes, toiletries, and snacks. Seeing a familiar face even if it was Deborah's made Betsy feel safe. For the first time in days, she tipped over the bottle of her feelings and let it gush all over her pastor's wife.

"Oh, dear, I'm so sorry. Let me see what we can do."

"Ya wud help me? Ya been so kind already. But I gotta have a house if I'm gonna get da kids back. Dey may be brats, but I miss dem."

"Don't worry about it all right now. Something will work out. Take it one day at a time, okay?" Deborah touched her arm gently and patted her hand. "I need to run, but I'll be back in a few days. In the meantime, we will pray about your situation."

Betsy nodded and waved as she went through the double doors.

~

When Deborah got home, she sat quietly for a long while, stunned. *Has Betsy accepted me as her friend? God, she is carrying a heavy load. Underneath her tough exterior is someone crying out for affection and acceptance. Would You show me how to demonstrate Your love to her?*

Then an idea came to her like a flash of lightning. *I could mass message my contacts list and post on the church's social media page for an emergency meeting. What I can't do by myself, a community can pitch in and help me.*

God, this is a huge problem and only You can open hearts to bring forth this miracle for Betsy and her family. Thank you for the little bit of a crack in her exterior armor. You are the One who can make this happen.

In a few short hours, people from all over town gathered in the fellowship hall in response to her message.

Deborah cleared her throat. "The Freemans need a miracle. Betsy told me the county health inspector condemned their house, and she lost her job. With less than 60 days left in the women's shelter, she needs a miracle. Their family may be among the least of these that the Bible talks about. How do we as Christians love the unlovable? Do we shove them out the door and tell them "God bless you" and go our merry way? Or do we like Jesus get down where they live, roll up our sleeves and get to work? Right now, is a crucial time for the family and we must put our personal feelings aside and be the church by showing compassion and unconditional love to the Freemans.

Until Betsy's situation improves, she will not get her children back. Is there anyone who could go to the property and look it over? Find out what the county officials are talking about."

Brennan Singleton raised his hand. "My neighbor is a contractor. I'll ask him."

"Thanks." Deborah glanced down at her scribbled pages on the legal pad.

She continued, "The Freemans need us now. How would Jesus want us to respond? Can we band together to get the job done?"

Miz Pennington stood shakily to her feet. "I know dis family, and we need to battle our way to glory for them. They are the lost sheep of this church, and we gotta see them brought into the kingdom of God."

Deborah interrupted her. "We are about to pray. Would you like to lead us?"

"Of course." Her cane thumped down hard to emphasize her approval. "Oh, dear God, the Freemans need You or they're going to be all destroyed...."

When Miz Pennington finished praying, her cane thumped again. It was like she sent God an air mail prayer.

~

When the group met again later, Brennan reported, "We cannot salvage the Freeman house. The only thing holding that place together is duct tape and termites holding hands."

"What can we do?" Darrell James interrupted.

"We need a workday on Saturday. Anyone who has free time between now and then, please let me know. Dial your contacts. Go on social media. You can even invite the Lutherans and Methodists across town." He chuckled dryly. "So much work, and so little time to pull off this miracle for the Freemans, so we need to muster up everyone we can."

"What kind of work needs to be done?" Frederick Howard piped up.

"The place looks like the plains of Africa. Generations of snakes and other creepy crawlers live in the thigh-high grass. We hope to find someone with a brush hog to mow it down. The overgrown bushes and trees need major attention to make them attractive again. Then, the basement foundation, if you can call it that, is stones stacked dryly on top of one another. No mortar within a country mile of the place."

"Tell you what," Deborah interrupted. "Why don't we start a Help the Freemans Campaign and appeal to the community-at-large? I'll talk to the Ministerial Association and Habitat for Humanity to see what they can do. In the meantime, spread the word. We'll see you all on Saturday."

At the Freeman fundraisers, nobody concerned themselves with race or church affiliation.

The Baptist youth group did car washes in their parking lot and raised a lot of money for the Freeman fund. Methodists hit the street corners with baked goods, and hosted spaghetti dinners in their fellowship hall. The Lutherans held rummage sales. The Catholics could not be outdone with their contributions of clothing, furniture, and household items.

Donations poured in from every church denomination. Deborah and the army of volunteers organized everything neatly in the church basement, stacking them in boxes up to the ceiling.

Contributed clothes past their use-by date found a second life as crazy quilts to line the family's beds. Classes at school adopted the Freeman household as the Spring project and held canned food drives. Closer to the farm, the men arrived with their tractors and lawn equipment, and tamed the jungle the Freemans called a yard.

Neighborhood ladies baked up such an enormous mountain of casseroles that there was a shortage of foil pans at the Family Dollar store for a week.

One could sense God's Presence hovering over the town like a mother hen protecting her chicks. Everyone forgot grudges. Denomination didn't matter. Neighbors helped each other with joy, and they came together to bring happiness to the Freeman's home. All great and small shared alike, and, for one second, as Pastor Johnson remarked one Sunday morning in the middle of this festival of caring, "all are of one accord."

10 God, Way Up Dere In Da Sky

Betsy sat with her eyeballs glued to the television as the local reporter told her story. She jumped up and yelled at the screen. "Dat's right, ya tell dem. All da men need ta stop tippin' da bottle and beatin' up da family. It ain't right now, is it? Just cuz I'm Betsy Freeman, da woman who done lives on da other side of da tracks, don't mean dat I ain't gotta keep my mouth shut about bein' hurt and all."

The TV presenter added, "If you want to contribute to Help the Freemans' Campaign, please call the number listed on the screen."

My miracle could come yet if'n God way up dere in da sky can hear me!

~

The angels in human form began their quest to prove to Betsy Freeman that "da God way up dere in da sky" heard her prayers and started unfolding the miraculous turn of events for her family.

~

Later, when Deborah arrived at the women's

shelter again, Betsy sat slumped over on the side of the bed chewing her fingernails to the quick. *Bite. Spit. Repeat.*

"Is everything okay, Betsy?"

"I'm worried sick about Hailey. She's gonna think I'm mad at her. Doctors say I have ta wait two more weeks before I can drive. Could ya take me ta see her?"

"I'll call the caseworker to make sure it is okay. It will only take a minute."

It's sad when I gotta ask ta see my flesh and blood. Da dumb gov'mint. Betsy sighed.

Returning inside, Deborah happily declared, "I got permission. Come on. I want to show you something first, though."

"What?"

"It's a big surprise."

Hopefully, it's good. I don't like bad ones. Betsy thought as she slid off her bed, smoothed the wrinkles, then slipped on her shoes.

"What are we doin' at da church?" Betsy asked as they descended the stairs and headed down the hall. *Dis better not be a waste of my time.*

They paused at the door of the largest Sunday School room. "Go ahead, open it." Deborah encouraged.

When Betsy stepped inside, she squalled so loudly that everyone upstairs came running.

"Is everything all right down here?" Pastor Johnson asked, all out of breath.

"Is all dis stuff for me and da family? I had no idee dat people would do dis." Betsy wiped her eyes.

"Folks around here love you and wanted to help your family start over again." Deborah hugged her as the others quietly slipped away.

"How'd dey know what ta get for us?"

"God told them."

"Dat was nice of Him when I don't know Him dat much."

"God knows everything."

"Oh look. Dere's clothes and stuff for da kids and us grownups. Might be a while before Thomas needs his things."

Deborah opened the next door. Betsy looked around with her mouth dragging on the floor. "We got unused furniture and everythin'. Hope dey got rid of dat nasty couch."

Betsy opened the upright freezer door. "We won't go hungry again. Dis is all too much. Why would people do dis for us?"

"Because Jesus loves you, and so do we, Betsy Freeman."

On the way to see Hailey, Betsy sat quietly thinking about what had just happened. Finally, she broke the silence. "Do ya think God way up dere in da sky would love someone as nasty as me? I don't fit in anywhere. People are mean ta me cuz I don't treat dem da way I should. Do ya think I can be one of God's people? Ya know, da kind dat is nice and loves people like ya do. After everythin' I done, I don't deserve anythin' from God."

"That's the whole idea, Betsy. None of us do. Just like you could have never done all of what was just given for you back there when you were stuck. You didn't get help until you asked for it. It is the same with the bad that we have done. We can't take care of the mess ourselves.

"None of us deserve the goodness of God, but it's offered as a gift. All you must do is ask."

"Ya mean dat? I ain't gotta go down front ta da altar and cry for an hour den stand up and say somethin'. Pap Fallon wanted people ta do dat but dere weren't any change. Dey still acted like bad people and fooled da preacher. I don't wanna do dat."

"You don't have to. You can ask Him to come into your heart here and now. I'll help you if you need it."

"I don't got da words ta say."

"Just talk to Him like you are talking to me. I'll help you if you need it."

"God, way up dere in da sky. I need help. I don't deserve nothin' good cuz of me actin' like da devil all da time. Could ya send Jesus ta my heart so I can be happy? I'm a miserable ole soul full of ugly stuff. Can ya help me start over? I'm sorry for all da terrible things I done. Amen."

Betsy's countenance changed. Joy replaced the sadness and pain that she carried for so long. She was still bawling from the birthing into the Kingdom of God.

"Welcome to the family, Betsy." Deborah wiped her eyes as they pulled into the hospital parking lot.

"I can forgive now." Betsy said as she closed her car door and walked through the hospital doors.

Betsy practically danced into Hailey's room with Deborah by her side. Traces of tears still stained the cheeks of both women.

"Hi. Mama, I was worried 'bout ya. Somethin's different. What happened to ya?"

"Ya remember that long talk we had bout forgiveness?"

"Yeah."

"I've found what Joseph did. God way up dere in da sky forgived my bad stuff, and I'm so happy."

"Good for you, Mama, but I ain't doing dat any time soon." Hailey scowled.

Betsy's mind flashed back to the night she saw Hailey knocked out cold on the floor. *If she hadn't stopped Thomas, den I'd be deader dan a doornail. Duty called; Hailey answered.*

Overwhelmed. Betsy shook her head, then hugged her daughter. "I love ya, Hailey."

She smiled. "It's so good to see ya, Mama."

~

On Saturday morning, as the sun peeked over the horizon, Betsy watched as a steady stream of cars turned into her driveway. *Dere's a lotta people comin' ta help da family. Dey cut da grass and cleaned up da yard. Now I can see da purty flowers and everythin'. Thank Ya, God, way up in da sky.*

Betsy buzzed around here and there like a bee searching for pollen. She stopped and sniffed. *OOH! Dat's cinnamon rolls. My fave.* She followed her nose to the tables set up in the barn. It seemed like miles of goodies going from one end to the other.

After they ate, Miz Pennington grabbed the megaphone. "Thank ya, everybody for comin.' Now, let's pray." Her authoritative voice rang out. Men removed their hats, and every eye closed because there'd be a reckoning with Miz Pennington for peeking around. She'd call them out during her prayer. "Oh, dear Lord, we're here today to help the Freemans. Ya know how much they need ya. Please keep everybody safe as we work. Amen. Now, let's get to it." *Thump!*

Her cane hit the ground.

Soon, everyone was about their business. Betsy and a small group of ladies grabbed boxes and headed up to the attic to sort and re-pack the salvageable items. Dust covered everything like a thick blanket. They could hear varmints scurrying and scampering to hide. Bare light bulbs lent their spooky glow to the group's tasks. After a while, Betsy stopped. "Ladies, I found somethin'."

"What is it?" echoed through the cobwebs and dust collection.

"Letters. Dey're still sealed up. Da same address is in da left corner. Caroline Freeman. Who's she? Thomas said his mama was dead, but dat's not true. Whatever, he needs ta read dese. Dere may be a key ta his problems here. Preacher man can take dem ta him when he goes to see him." She crawled down the rickety steps.

At lunchtime, Betsy grabbed the megaphone. "It's time ta eat." Her voice reverberated over all parts of the farm. People came out of the woodwork and appeared at the tables as ravenous as wolves. All the casserole dishes, fried chicken, meatloaf, pork ribs, and dessert containers sat empty of any food. Despite denomination or race, everyone visited noisily until a dump truck's horn blew and the head contractor announced, "The house is empty; the electricity, water, and gas lines are off. Please stay away from the caution tape because it is time for the walls to come down."

Betsy grabbed the megaphone again. "Ya'll heard da guy. Get back unless ya wanna wake up in da hospital with wires stickin' outta yer head."

Excavators grabbed gigantic bites of rotted wood,

shingles, and years' worth of debris and smacked the dump trucks' beds with a thunderous BOOM! Enormous clouds of dust swirled upward, settling on anything in their path. The trucks headed down the hill toward the city dump, taking the termites and strands of duct tape along with them.

Betsy grabbed the megaphone again. In her loud and off-key voice, she sang, "Joshua Fit da Battle of Jericho… and da Walls Came Tumbling down…"

11   The Letters

The following Monday, Betsy went to the doctor for her six-week checkup after emergency surgery. She mumbled under her breath. "I've been sittin' here so long you'd think I was hatchin' a bunch of eggs."

The nurse opened the door. "Caroline Freeman."

Betsy's head came up so fast you could hear the bones crack across the room. She jumped to her feet. "Wait a sec, lady. Yer Caroline? Are ya Thomas's mom?"

The dark-haired woman turned. "Yes. Do you know him?"

The nurse snapped her gum impatiently.

"He told me ya was six feet under." Betsy huffed. Why'd he lie ta me?"

"Excuse me, ladies, the doctor is waiting." *Snap! Pop!*

Caroline pulled out a piece of paper and a pen, then swiftly wrote her number. "Call me later. We have a lot to talk about."

When they met the next afternoon, Betsy's questions were like bullets shot by a machine gun.

When she took a breath, all was silent around them in the park. Betsy paused in her excitement.

"I don't know if I can answer everything, but let's start at the beginning. I married Thomas's dad when I was barely eighteen."

"Well, why didn't ya stick around and raise him up proper like?" Betsy blurted.

Caroline looked at her watch. "The long story short is that my in-laws hated me. One night after they drank the biggest jug of moonshine I'd ever seen; Thomas's grandpappy grabbed a rifle and threatened me within an inch of my life if I showed up at the farm again. I stuffed a suitcase with as much as I could and ran for it. I couldn't take Thomas with me. I still get flashbacks of that night with Grandpappy Freeman peppering my car with bullets as I sped down the driveway, fleeing for my life." She paused a moment, and her eyes grew wide with the memory of that night.

"Every birthday and Christmas I sent cards and letters, but I never got a reply. He may not have known about them because the Freeman bunch was as ornery as the day is long."

"Why haven't I seen ya before?"

"Because I live in another town."

"Dat makes sense." Betsy sighed. "Do ya love Thomas?"

"With all my heart. I never stopped. He doesn't understand it because neither his grandparents nor his daddy showed him love. I hope he finds out someday that I never gave up on him."

"The letters could help."

"What do you mean?"

"I found a shoebox full of dem in da attic. Dey're

sealed up tight. I gave dem ta Preacher man cuz he visits da drunk in jail."

"Why'd you call him that?"

"He don't treat me nor da kids proper-like cuz he drinks like a fish."

"I'm sorry to hear that. He's following in his father's footsteps."

~

Thomas sat in his cell craving another drink. Rage boiled inside him like a fire in a furnace. He cursed and banged his fists on the cement block wall until his knuckles were swollen and bloody. Angrily, he wiped the blood on his uniform. *Can't believe what Betsy done ta me. Dis is all her fault. She don't wanna see me. I got one free phone call, and she wudn't take it. What's wrong with dat woman? Just wait til I get my hands on her again. She'll be sorrier dan a hound a'beggin' for vittles.*

Early the next morning, before the sun turned the sky pink, the guard opened Thomas's cell door. "Come on, Freeman, the judge sent an order for you to start detox this morning. Let's go."

"But I ain't had nothin' ta eat. Least at home Betsy brought strong coffee and a piece of toast."

"Shut up, Freeman. You'll get something in a little bit."

The guards loaded Thomas in the waiting van, and they headed down the road to another part of the compound. The big sign at the end of the drive read, RIFTWOOD SOBER LIVING PROGRAM. The van pulled up and stopped under the portico. "Okay, here we are, Freeman."

"What's dis place?" Thomas jumped down out of

the van.

"Detox hospital."

I'm not taken in by it. Looks as spooky and empty as I feel inside. His stomach growled in response.

Hope da guard heard dat. I'm gettin' hangry!

Thomas was already feeling the withdrawal symptoms from having no alcohol yesterday. *Am I really dis bad a drunk dat I can't go for one day without a drink? It's all Betsy's fault. If she weren't such a nag, den I wudn't drink so much.*

That night, Thomas mumbled like a monkey in the jungle, jumping in and out of bed and chasing the elusive dancing animals all over the room. *Clank! Clunk! Bang! Thump!* All night long.

Between his sleepless night and the tremors, His nerves were about to snap like the last thread of a frayed rope. Depression set in, wrapping its icy fingers around his heart. *Detox is hard. Somethin' has ta change, or I'm never gonna get out of dis loony bin.*

In his daily counseling sessions, Thomas learned that he had a choice to forgive Grandpappy and Granny Freeman or not. But if he didn't let go of the pain they caused him and remain bitter; he would not make any progress toward healing. *What's a man to do?* He felt trapped in a tar pit and saw no hope for the future. That's why he found himself on a suicide watch.

Betsy and da kids wud be better off without me but I ain't brave enough to do da job. Somethin' always stops me. He needed help. That is when his eyes fell on the card which Pastor Johnson gave him.

Wudn't hurt, wud it?

He used his one weekly call to dial the number on Pastor Johnson's card. When he answered, Thomas spilled his guts. "I don't got no hope, but I can't kill myself." He started to sob.

"Would you want me to visit you?"

"Yeah," Thomas dried his tears and sighed deeply. "I'm not at da jail. Da judge sent me ta Riftwood."

"OK. I'll be there soon."

~

When Pastor Johnson pulled up at the Riftwood Sober Living building, he shivered. *No wonder Thomas feels trapped.* A metal fence with sharp barbed wire surrounded the grounds which were unkempt and messy. *This place needs some rehabilitation itself.*

Pastor Johnson greeted him, and they sat down together at a small table beside a large dirty window. *Thomas appears gaunt and shaky. It must be the meds he's on.*

~

Thomas began talking right away. "We gotta go to counselin' here. Dese psychology people think dere so smart standin' up dere jabberin' bout feelin' down and not forgivin'. Dey sound like a 'skita buzzin' round da ears. I wanna slap dem ta shut dem up, but I'd go straight back ta da jail. Dey say we ain't gonna get better until we learn ta forgive. Whadd'ya reckon dere sayin'?"

"Do you know what forgiveness is, Thomas?"

"Nah."

"Forgiving others is to drop all the bitterness at people for what they have done to us and letting go of grudges toward them. " Pastor Johnson opened his Bible and read Jesus's parable the servant who wouldn't forgive. "If we don't forgive others, then God won't forgive us."

Thomas interrupted. " Ya think God wud help me with dat?"

"Of course, He will."

"How'd ya know dat?"

"Because my dad was an alcoholic, and he treated me the same way that you have treated your family. It was a challenging thing to do, but when I let go of all that hurt, God sent peace to my heart. I learned to forgive and move on with my life."

"Hearin' ya talkin' helps me know ya understand da struggles I face every day. Ya been dere and knows what needs ta happen ta me. Like da counselor said, I gotta forgive my grandpappy and granny. I can't do dat by myself."

"No, you can't. But Jesus can. Do you want to talk to Him?"

"I ain't never done dat before," Thomas replied.

They bowed their heads. For the first time in his life Thomas prayed. "God in Heaven, dis old drunk needs ya ta wipe away all da wrong stuff I done…da drinkin,' da beatin', da cussin'. Da pastor here said Ya cud help me forgive other people cuz Ya forgive me. Can Ya do dat?" He paused. "Do I say Amen now?"

The minister nodded.

"Amen." Thomas 'shouted with tears streaming down his face.

Pastor Johnson smiled and stood. "You have my number. Call me if you need me again. Oops! I almost forgot; Betsy gave me these to give to you."

"What ya talkin' bout?"

"The letters that you never got from your mama are in this box. You have some reading to do."

"Can ya tell my wife what happened today?"

"I certainly will." Pastor Johnson smiled.

After the pastor left, Thomas carefully opened each letter. My Dear Son: I'm not sure if you understand how much I love you. I miss you every day... He slowly read the contents, stumbling over the words. He breathed her name. *Mama, I never knew.* Her love filled those tiny fissures of his rocky heart. They wooed him out of the shadows of hatred and bitterness.

Caroline Freeman's love for him made itself clear on the pages of the letters

Is dis what true love feels like?

Then the reality of what happened caused Thomas's fury to increase like a prairie fire. *How dare Granny and Grandpappy do dis ta me! Grandpappy always kept a loaded .22 by da front door and would kill her if she stepped foot on da property. Mama didn't deserve dat.*

He put his head down and wept uncontrollably for a long time. His unyielding heart melted like butter. Instead of the anger a moment ago, he felt his mama's love surrounded him, but there seemed to be another Presence. *God, is dat Ya talkin' ta me?*

Yes, Thomas. You can let it all go now. They can't hurt you anymore. They are dead and gone, but you are still here dealing with the aftermath of your past. What would your children say about your treatment of them? You have a chance to start over. They don't. If you are willing to, I will help you mend your past so that the future will be better than your past.

Can ya do dat, God?

Of course, I can. We start over today. You are my child and I love you.

12 Hailey Gets Out of the Hospital.

Discharge Day. Finally. Hailey waited impatiently for Felicity to arrive. *Foster care can't be as bad as dis borin' place. At least I'll be with my brother and sisters.* She started chewing her fingernails. I don't wanna be bullied as a foster kid.

She cocked her head. *Tap! Tap! Rata-tat-tat! Yep, the high heels are comin' dis way.*

Felicity waltzed into her room and laid a shopping bag on her bed. "Got you an outfit to wear out of here. Hurry now. I don't have all day."

Hailey slipped into the bathroom, and swiftly shucked off the gown that had been her entire wardrobe for the past weeks. *Good riddance!*

Hailey opened the bathroom door. "Ta-da. Thanks for da clothes."

Felicity nodded and picked up her discharge papers, then skimmed them. "Physical therapy starts next Monday. Be there."

"K." Hailey put on her neck brace and grabbed her

backpack. They raced to the elevator, and then burst through the double exit doors. She breathed in deeply and exhaled the stale hospital air. AHH. *Dat's so much better.*

She climbed into Felicity's sports car. *Nice ride.*

They zoomed down the highway at speeds well above the posted limit. "You're gonna get caught doin' dis." Hailey grasped the armrests for all she was worth silently hoping that they didn't crash and end up right back in the hospital.

Finally, they pulled up to a nice suburban home. "Good luck, Hailey. Call me if you need anything." Felicity handed her a business card and a small suitcase. " I got a few necessary things for you." She hopped back into her car and rocketed out of sight.

~

"Hailey's here!" Kaylee yelled when she turned the knob and pulled the door open. Her little sister's excitement made her head pound out a rhythm like torrential rain on a tin roof. She squinted as the pain shot to her forehead and ricocheted through her skull at the speed of light. Hailey slid down the wall to the floor and rubbed her temples to release the tension.

Mrs. Baker intervened. "Quiet down. You can talk more to Hailey after a while."

It would have been nice to stay with Vanessa, but at least Mrs. Baker isn't a stranger. I remember her givin' out candy at da end of Sunday School.

Mrs. Baker led the teen to her room and handed her two pain relief tablets and a glass of water. "These should help."

Hailey sat down on the bed and opened her backpack. "Dese are da appointments dat I got." She handed the Discharge Summary to Mrs. Baker.

"Ok. We'll deal with all of that after your nap. I'll call you when supper is ready."

"Thanks." Hailey yawned. *Who knew gettin' outta da hospital took so much energy?*

Hailey did not know how long she slept, but the sun was setting when she awoke to a persistent soft knock on her door.

"Suppertime."

Hailey sat up and rubbed her eyes. "Comin'."

When she got to the table, her siblings were sitting quietly, waiting for her. Their hands and faces were clean, and their hair had been combed. *What have ya done with my brother and sisters? Have da Martians landed, and body swapped dem? Somethin's a bit fishy here.*

Hailey almost missed the cue as everyone else bowed their heads and said grace. *We never did dat at home.*

As soon as the prayer finished, Hailey looked up. Mrs. Baker helped Kaylee with serving her plate then she passed the steaming bowls around the table.

I'm gonna die if'n I don't get food into my stomach. Haven't eaten since breakfast. Hailey reached, grabbed, and sloshed the food as she did before. *Snatch while da gettin's good.*

"Hailey. Please sit down. We'll pass the dishes around the table to you."

She lowered her head, embarrassed because she didn't know what to do. When her plate was full, Hailey stuffed her mouth as quickly as she could.

"Slow down, Hailey, take time to enjoy your food. You'll get a tummy ache from eating too fast. There's plenty of food on the table. You'll not go away hungry."

"Sorry, Mrs. Baker. I have been livin' on a hospital diet for weeks now. Dis is da best meal ever!"

After the meal, her siblings asked to be excused and then did their chores. Jenny and Kaylee went into the kitchen to do the dishes. Peter emptied the trash cans, then the vacuum started up as he cleaned the living room floor.

I can't believe dat dese are my siblin's. Dey never helped at home. Wonder how long dis'll last.

Mrs. Baker approached. "Once you settle in, I'll teach you how to do the laundry."

"Okay."

"Come. I have something to show you." They walked into Mrs. Baker's office. "A letter came for you."

Hailey sat down on a comfortable chair and stared at the return address. *Dis is from Judge Paxton. What'd I do now?*

Hailey's heart thumped in her ears as she slit open the letter. She exhaled. "Phew! I thought I was in trouble. Dad's sentencin' is Friday, and da judge wants me to say somethin.' I got plenty ta tell dat ole drunk."

"Make your words sweet because you might have to eat them someday." Mrs. Baker lightly brushed her shoulder.

Hailey stood and mumbled. "I wanna go ta my room."

"Okay. Let me know if you need anything."

~

A knock sounded on the back door. Mrs. Baker answered it and escorted Vanessa to Hailey's room.

"Hi!" She greeted Hailey with a gentle hug. "Did you think that I wouldn't find you? Schoolwork has a GPS installed; you know."

Hailey laughed.

"Are you ready to get down to business?" Vanessa slid her chair next to Hailey's.

"I guess. Then ya can tell me all bout what's goin' on at school." They opened their books and got busy.

x+3=y-2. *HUH?*

13 The Sentencing Hearing

Friday morning was chaotic. After breakfast, Mrs. Baker sent the younger Freeman children off to get dressed while she swiftly washed the dishes. Hailey dried them and put them away, then she went to her room.

Mrs. Baker raced around making sure that the children looked their best. She combed Jenny's brown hair and Kaylee's strawberry-blonde curls. She finished their hair by adding big pretty bows to match their outfits. Then, she helped Peter learn to tie his tie.

"Hailey, everyone is waiting for you." Mrs. Baker called.

"Be right dere." She gulped down two pain killers and put her neck brace on, then pranced down the hall in the most beautiful dress ever. *I never felt dis way before. Most of my clothes were ratty and ugly. Now, I dress like a princess instead of my frumpy mama.*

The Freeman children raced to the van. "All

aboard and fasten your seat belts." She backed down the driveway and across town to the courthouse. When she pulled into the parking lot, Mrs. Baker's van crept at a snail's pace. Crowds of people waited outside the building, crammed the entrance, and spilled out into the vehicle bays like it was a Black Friday sale.

Where did these people come from?

"Okay, kiddos, keep your eyes open for a parking place." Mrs. Baker glanced into her rearview mirror.

"I gotta go potty," Kaylee whined.

"Sorry, Honey, you'll have to wait a little bit."

Kaylee wriggled in her seat.

"Dere's a place." Peter pointed to a spot one aisle over.

Mrs. Baker slowly wove through the crowd and whipped into the spot. Instantly, big fuzzy microphones stuck themselves to her window like woolly worms.

You've got to be kidding me!

Turning to the children, she warned, "Ignore them or no Pizza Palace afterward. Got it?"

"Yeah!" All responded.

She rolled her window down a tiny bit. "Go away!" She closed the gap then dialed the courthouse security line. Shortly, several officers rushed out and escorted the family inside.

After their Ladies' Room stop, Mrs. Baker and the girls joined Peter, who sat on a bench swinging his legs. Immediately, Bailiff Simpson whisked them into the courtroom; locked the doors, then led them to their seats. "This is where you will stand when you speak to your daddy. You can help him make a big choice, either go to prison or stay in detox intervention."

"What's intavenshun?" Kaylee's big blue eyes

looked up at him.

"Your dad has been at a special hospital to make him not want liquor anymore. Then, he will go to a different place to help him get a job. If he doesn't choose to stay in detox intervention, he won't be able to get out of prison until you are all grown."

"I don't like dat!" Kaylee, Daddy's little pet, stamped her foot and scowled.

Soon, the side door opened, and Joseph entered wearing a bright orange jumpsuit with chains around his wrists and legs. They rattled together. *Clank! Clunk!*

"Joey!" Four-year-old Kaylee, in her dark green ruffled dress, ran to him and wrapped her little arms around his legs. "I miss ya. Why ya got cuffs on?"

"Because I did somethin' bad."

"Honest?" Tears welled up in Kaylee's eyes.

"Ah, now. It's okay. I'm goin' home again soon."

"Ya promise?"

Joseph changed the subject. "Ya look so purty."

She twirled around and her strawberry-blonde curls bounced. Seeing her mother, she skipped back the aisle to Betsy.

When she saw Joseph, Betsy wept.

"Don't cry, Mama. It's okay. Joey's comin' home soon."

Betsy pulled her little daughter close to her breast and tried to put on a brave face for her through her tears. "Mama will be okay," she said, mustering up the courage from somewhere deep within to comfort her scared little girl. Betsy, too, felt consoled by Kaylee's kindness.

Thank ya, God way up in da sky for my little girl. She makes me feel better.

Betsy looked up at the clock above the judge's desk and drew in a shaky breath. *It's time.* The knot in her stomach tightened. *I shouldn't have done dis ta Thomas. But how else was I gonna stop da hittin'?*

In her heart she heard the whisper. *"The best reason is curled up beside you."*

"Yer right, God way up in da sky."

~

Judge Paxton halted while Bailiff Simpson announced him to the audience. "All rise for The Honorable Judge Henry Paxton. The court is now in session." He turned to the official, "Your Honor, this is case 14729003, The State vs. Thomas Freeman."

"Thank you, Bailiff. You all may be seated. Good morning, everyone. I have asked Thomas Freeman's family to speak what's on their minds." Judge Paxton turned to address Thomas. "For once in your life, young man, listen to them."

Thomas fidgeted with his hands, shuffled his feet, while he lowered his eyes, and peeked sideways at his children. *God, I know I done dem all wrong, and I deserve what I'm gonna hear. Help me!*

The judge nodded at Hailey. "State your name for the court, then you may begin."

Her dress swished as she stepped to the microphone, adjusted her neck brace, then cleared her throat. "Hi! I'm Hailey Freeman. As ya'll know dat I was in da hospital for three weeks cuz of what my dad did ta me. I could've been paralyzed. For your info, Dad, I gotta deal with headaches da rest of my life. I'm so mad da I cud spit nails."

"Mom got hurt, too. She lost her job, and we lost da house all cuz of whatcha' done. Us kids are in foster care, so who knows when we can get ta be with Mama again. Da family's cursed cuz of drink. Dat's not da worst of it. We cud grow up without a dad. Is dat whatcha want? Drinkin' don't help ya any. It turns ya into dis beast we don't know. Daddy, it's time to do da right thing for da family for once."

Hailey's head throbbed, and she choked on her tears as she walked back to her seat. Mrs. Baker held her in her arms until Hailey stopped shaking.

Thomas hung his head. Big tears dropped onto his ragged shoes. *Don't be mad at me, Hailey. I didn't mean it. God, help me ta fix dis.*

"Hi, I'm Joseph Freeman." He turned to face his father. "Look at me, Dad. I'm in chains, just like ya are. Bet dose were words ya never wanted ta hear. I headed down da same path yer on." The shackles rattled as he lifted his hands for emphasis. "It wasn't right what I done, but I was tryin' ta be a man and provide for da family cuz ya weren't. Dat nasty bottle yer addicted to left nothin' for da basic needs of da family. I sold weed ta get food and shoes. It was a dumb way ta earn money, but I learned my lesson. If'n ya didn't have dat love of drink; things would be better. My vote is for ya to stay in da Sober Living Program so we can start over as a family.

"I hated ya, but Jesus helped me ta become a better person, and I can't detest ya no more. I got a second chance. By forgiving ya, I found peace. I want that for ya, too."

What kind of monster have I become? No more, God, I can't take it. I didn't know how dey felt.

Peter pulled at his shirt collar and buttoned his suit coat. "I'm Peter Freeman. Dad," his voice crackled.

"If'n I was in yer shoes; I'd choose to stay where ya can get help. I saw what ya done ta Mama and Hailey, and it makes me mad enough ta kick a cat, but dat's stoopin' ta yer level. Ya can do way better as a dad. Ya can be so fun sometimes, but not when yer drinkin.' So, it makes sense ta lay off da booze, and come home ta us. We need ya."

What is Peter going to become if I'm locked away for his growing-up years? I'm a terrible dad ta dem.

"Hi, I'm Jenny Freeman." Her starched violet dress rustled as she twisted this way and that. She enjoyed the momentary spotlight. Then she clearly said, " I'm glad yer gettin' sober, Daddy. It will make ya happy."

I don't know what happiness is. God, can ya help me with dat?

Kaylee walked up the aisle to Hailey and grabbed her hand tightly. When she turned to look at Thomas, she burst into tears. She loved her daddy, and her raw emotions showed clearly. Hailey calmed her. "This is Kaylee Freeman," she introduced her sister.

Kaylee spoke one word. "Intavenshun." She burst into tears again. Mrs. Baker rushed from her seat, picked her up, and carried her back to the first row of chairs.

What have I done to my baby girl?

Sniffles encircled the courtroom.

His wife spoke next. "I'm Betsy Freeman. Thomas, dis ain't a walk in da park for any of us. Yer drinkin' is tearin' da family apart. Enuff's enuff! I seen what it done ta yer dad and my mama. I can't let it happen ta someone I love. I'm puttin' my foot down. Ya ain't gonna beat us no more. Take dis chance and stay in da sober place. Ya got a year ta think bout yer choices.

Come back ta da kids and me a better man. Can ya do dat, Thomas?" Betsy's heartbroken sobs could be heard way in the back of the courtroom.

Thomas hung his head. *My wife, I can't believe ya still love me I done. God, I don't deserve her.*

When she was through, a stranger stood and walked to the microphone.

Wait a minute! I know dis woman. Where'd I seen her before?

She looked directly at Thomas as if she knew him. The audience hushed; their whispering hung in mid-air as if suspended by a thread.

She turned and addressed Judge Paxton. "Thank you for this opportunity. Your Honor, I am Caroline Freeman, Thomas's mother."

She turned to him. "Thomas, I have always loved you, and want what is best for your family. Your wife needs a companion to help her raise your offspring. They need you to break this generational chain of alcohol addiction, otherwise, they will end us as drunkards and violent offenders. Stay in detox, then together we can work through your past, and change the future for the family. Your daddy did not choose intervention and look how he ended up. I don't want that for you. Take this chance to do what's right for your family."

Mama! Grandpappy Freeman told me ya was dead. He gritted his teeth in anger.

When Caroline turned to return to her seat, it looked like a roomful of Venus Fly Traps with gaping jaws awaiting their prey.

"The court will take a brief recess while I meet with the attorneys in my chambers." Judge Paxton stood and those in attendance followed suit.

When they returned, the magistrate turned to Thomas. "You've heard your family pleading with you to stay in detox for your addiction to alcohol. What do you have to say?"

Thomas tearfully rasped, "First off, I'm sorry ta da family for what I done. Dey spoke da truth. I'm a monster. I started drinkin' after workin' from dawn ta dusk. Grandpappy's voice echoes in my head all da time, tellin' me dat I'm worthless. I'm stuck in a deep dark pit cuz I can't change myself, so Ya Honor, my choice…" He paused. The entire audience sat on the edge of their seats, hardly daring to breathe. Thomas raised his head and looked at the judge, "I choose ta stay in da Sober Living Program." *God help me!*

Betsy stood and shouted. "Way to go, Thomas!"

The judge pounded his gavel on the desk. "Order in the court. Very well, Thomas. I will give you a deferred adjudication, which means that if you take one drop of alcohol, prison time awaits. It will be the full twenty years that the State recommended. This is a profoundly serious offer. Learn from your past ways and make something of yourself. We don't want to see you as another statistic in the obituaries.

Thomas shivered.

The judge shuffled the papers in front of him. "First, you are to go back to Riftwood County Sober Living Program for sixty days, then on to Brock's Home to learn job skills. Next, you will do three hundred hours of Community Service. Finally, you must attend AA weekly for the rest of your life. Do you understand?"

"Yeah, Yer Honor. Thank ya for da chance. I

won't mess up."

"Good. So be it. Thomas Freeman, you made the right choice."

Turning to the officers, the judge firmly said, "Guards, take him back to the Riftwood County Sober Living Program." And the gavel dropped.

1 4   Leave Us Alone

As she promised, Mrs. Baker took the children to Pizza Palace right after the hearing. As soon as they found their seats, Felicity and Betsy opened the door, and the media circus followed them in like yipping puppies.

"What's going to happen to your family now that your husband has been taken away? What are you going to do now?" The questions peppered them as they entered the restaurant.

When Betsy turned around, they stopped in their tracks like children playing freeze tag. "Why don't ya'll go mind yer own business, and let me worry bout what's next for me and my kids? Ya'll are like tryin' ta get a cocklebur outta yer hair. And if'n ya'll don't stop, I'll call da police." Betsy hissed at them until they scattered like fall leaves in the wind.

"Hope dat works." Betsy joined the family for pizza. She looked around the table at her kiddos eating mannerly. *What's done happen to da young'uns? Hailey seems kinda quiet-like though. Wonder what's wrong with her.* Betsy slid across the bench closer to

Hailey.

"Is dere somethin' wrong?"

"I don't feel good, 'scuse me." Hailey slid out of the bench and made a beeline for the Ladies' Room. Her head throbbed out a rhythm of a drummer at a rock concert while her food fought like two alley cats in her stomach. Hailey crashed through the door and fell to her knees inside the first stall.

Mrs. Baker and Betsy followed her into the restroom and knelt on either side of her while Hailey surrendered her fight against nausea. Betsy put her arm across her shoulder. "Sorry, yer sick, Hailey. We need to get help." Hailey leaned her head against Betsy and prayed that the cramps would stop.

Mrs. Baker was already dialing 911 while Betsy stayed by Hailey's side until the ambulance took her and Felicity away.

Then, Mrs. Baker boxed up the leftover pizza, gathered the other children, and headed swiftly to the Emergency Room.

"I'll meet ya dere," Betsy called over her shoulder then slammed her car door shut.

~

Meanwhile, in Mrs. Baker's van, things began heating up into an argument.

"T'wasn't done eatin' da pizza. Stupid Hailey had ta ruin ev'rythin'. She gets all da attention round here." Peter grumbled.

Kaylee started crying. Yer bein' mean, Peter."

"Stop it! How'd ya like pukin' yer guts up into da pot? So, yer a little hungry, deal with it. When we get ta da hospital, ya cud eat another piece. Hailey can't. Yer just bein' selfish by makin' dis all about yerself. Grow up!" Jenny huffed. "Me and Hailey fight lots. But I'm gonna stick up for her when she can't help bein' so sick."

Mrs. Baker shook her head. "Jenny, you don't need to be quite so hard on your brother. Everyone is tired, and today was tough for all of us."

She glanced at Peter in the rear-view mirror. "We are going to have a chat when we get home." Mrs. Baker warned him, and she always came through with her promises.

Peter slid down deeper into his seat and sulked because he knew what that meant…extra chores for at the next two days if he was lucky. He wanted to kick Jenny or hit something, but he knew from experience how that would work out for him. *Man, Mrs. Baker's tough.*

When they arrived at the Emergency Room, the youngsters sat in the waiting area with Felicity and Betsy while Mrs. Baker visited Hailey. The little ones fidgeted on the hard chairs, bored out of their minds because there was nothing for them to do besides watch the clock.

In time, Kaylee crawled up in her mother's lap and fell asleep. Jenny sat with her head down, swinging her legs under the chair. Peter found himself in the corner with his lower lip big enough to set a rooster on.

It seemed like forever and a day before Mrs. Baker came back through the double doors. "Come," she motioned to the children, "Your sister needs to stay here overnight, so we can go home now." They woke up a very unhappy Kaylee and bundled her into her car seat. She turned her head to the side and fell asleep again.

No one spoke on the way home. It had been an exceptionally long day, and it was going to be even longer for Peter.

Once they were home, Mrs. Baker put a nighttime pull-up on Kaylee and changed her into her pajamas, tucked her in for the night, and kissed her cheek.

Jenny lay back on her bed reading a book for a school assignment. Mrs. Baker sat down on the side of the bed. Are you okay?"

"I'm mad at Peter for makin' a big to-do outta nothin'. Us girls fight, den it's all over. He's not dat way."

"First off, he is your brother, and you must understand that boys don't think like girls. You're an amazing support for your sister. You understand her better because you are a girl. Peter cares for Hailey, but he doesn't show it the same way you do.

When a boy gets upset, they lash out because society tells them that boys are too tough to break out in tears. Girls can cry for a while, then it's all over."

"Freemans don't cry. We break stuff."

Mrs. Baker bit her tongue. She wanted to say, *and how's that working out for your family?* She pulled Jenny close. "A glass can easily be broken and swept away. A heart can't be."

Jenny sat there quietly for a moment. "Dere's a lotta broken hearts in our house!"

"Change can happen in the next weeks or months. It's going to take time, love, and patience from all of us."

"Guess so." Jenny opened her book.

"Good night, Jenny. I'll see you in the morning. Remember it'll be Saturday, and it's your turn to pick a special activity to do after chores. Do you know what you want to do?"

"Not yet. It'll be a surprise."

"Okay, Sweetie. Don't stay up too late."

"I won't." Jenny yawned.

Mrs. Baker went downstairs. *Off to clean up some more broken glass.*

She sat down beside Peter. "Do you want to tell me what's going on?"

"Not really." Peter lowered his head.

Mrs. Baker persisted. " You have not been happy since Hailey got out of the hospital."

Peter mumbled something under his breath.

"Speak up, Peter. I haven't been able to hear that tone since 1993."

"It's not fair. It's Hailey dis and Hailey dat."

Mrs. Baker sighed deeply and shot a prayer heavenward. *Lord, give me wisdom to help this boy.*

Peter took her silence as permission to continue.

"Did ya have yer own kids?"

"Of course. I raised five of them and lots of foster kids along the way. Their pictures are all on the wall over there." She pointed to the living room.

"I thought dey were pics of some of yer students when ya taught school."

"After my husband passed away from a car accident, I wanted to keep helping children. But I didn't want to return to the classroom, so I decided to make a difference in as many children's lives as possible. That's why I do foster care.

"Each child is different and special in his own way. Every picture has a story. Some are happy and some are sad. Most are a bit of both."

Peter looked puzzled. "Like how?"

"See the boy in that picture?" She pointed to a sad young man with a hat pulled down over his bushy curls. Danny was a student of mine. He lived in a bad section of town. His parents were on drugs, and he got into that lifestyle in middle school. He spent some time in juvenile hall. By the time Danny got to me, he was a tough customer."

Peter was intrigued now. "What happened to him?"

"He ran away a couple times, and the police brought him back to me. Finally, he got to the end of his journey with drugs. He went to school to be a mechanic and runs the little shop on 15th street. He does all my oil changes."

"Sounds like Joseph. He's in juvie cuz of sellin' drugs."

"A bad chapter does not make a bad book, Peter. Joseph made wrong choices, but it doesn't mean he'll be that way forever. Joseph is getting the help he needs. He'll be back home before you know it."

"I miss him."

"I understand, buddy. It's perfectly normal to feel that way. You have a lot going on in your life."

"I'm sorry about what I said about Hailey. I didn't mean it."

"I know, Peter. If you ever want to talk about it, I'm here."

His shoulders slumped and it seemed like someone pulled the plug out. Pent-up tears poured down his cheeks.

It had to come out sometime. Mrs. Baker thought. She put her arm around his shoulders, but he resisted. "It shoulda been me, but I had ta get Mama outta Dad's way. I dream about it all da time."

"It's not your fault, Peter. You were so brave and did what you had to do to protect your Mama from harm. That's supposed to be a man's job, and you shouldn't feel bad. Not a lot of boys your age would've stepped in and done what you did. You're a hero to me, your sister, and to everyone else. Nothing can take that away."

"What about da bad dreams?"

"I can't make them go away, Peter. It's going to take time to heal your mind, just like it's going to take time for Hailey's head to get better."

Peter giggled.

Mrs. Baker looked at him strangely. "What's so funny?"

"Are ya sayin' we're both messed up in da head?"

They both laughed.

Thank you, Jesus. It's a breakthrough for Peter.

Mrs. Baker fixed him a cup of hot chocolate, and they sat at the table talking until way past his bedtime, but it was important for Peter to feel like he was being heard.

~

Back at the hospital, Felicity rode the elevator to the fifth floor and clomped down the hall to Hailey's room. "I thought you were done with this place." SCREECH! She dragged the chair across the waxed floor and plopped herself next to Hailey's bed.

Hailey did not answer her because her head hurt too much, and her stomach was ready to upend itself if she opened her mouth to speak. Felicity Wells's nasally, loud, and cheerful voice was hard to take without a headache.

~

Soon Dr. Bender entered the room. "You're suffering from a migraine brought on by stress. We want to be sure that nothing else is going on. We'll run a few tests to make sure. How's the nausea?"

Hailey made motions with her hands to indicate that her stomach was still upset.

"Okay. I'll give you another shot to help with that. Anything else?"

Maybe get rid of dis loud-mouthed bother.

As soon as the room became quiet again, she fell asleep, only waking up when the nurse placed her breakfast tray on her bedside table.

"Good morning, Miss Hailey. Time to step lively now. Your family will be here soon to take you home.

Hailey wolfed the food down and hurried to the bathroom to change. She sniffed the shirt. *EWW, smells like puke.*

Later, Mrs. Baker and her siblings peeked around her curtain. "Are you ready to go home?"

"Did ya bring fresh clothes?"

"Of course. Here you go."

Hailey sniffed the garments. *Ahh! Nice and clean. Mrs. Baker's so thoughtful.*

The next day was Sunday…time to see Mama. Mrs. Baker made them dress up to go to church. "Why can't we wear anythin' we want?" Peter complained.

"Because it is the Lord's Day, and we show respect to Him by dressing nicely." Peter wore neatly pressed slacks and a blue button-down shirt. When he looked in the mirror, he did not see stains nor holes in his shirt. His shoes were no longer two sizes too small cramping his toes. They wiggled freely inside clean socks instead of out in the air for everyone to see.

The girls' hair shone beautifully, and their clothes were clean and tidy. Jenny and Kaylee clutched their matching purses tightly. Mrs. Baker filled them with coins, handkerchiefs, and tiny finger dolls.

Hailey refused to be outshined. She sashayed in a cloud of ribbons and lace. Her blonde curls bounced as she pranced down the hall. Mrs. Baker stopped her at the door. "Ease up a little on the flounce there, girlie. We're going to church, not prom."

Hayley pouted a little. "A girl wants to look her best."

"Oh yeah? Since when?" Shot back Peter, preening at the mirror, trying to lay down one last errant strand of hair.

Hailey ignored his comment and turned to stare right at him.

"Oh yeah, since when indeed?" She repeated, mockingly.

Mrs. Baker rolled her eyes. *Typical sibling nonsense.*

When they arrived at church, the children tried to open their doors and race up the sidewalk like they habitually did. She locked them in with a flick of her wrist. "Oh no you don't," Mrs. Baker commanded. She had spent far too long scrubbing grass stains out of Peter's church pants from last week's "football" incident to let that happen again.

"We'll go up the sidewalk together in a group like a gentleman and ladies should. There will be no rushing the door and ignoring Pastor Johnson. Each of us will greet him properly, otherwise there'll be trouble.

Mrs. Baker could see a group of teenage boys

starting to form over in the side lawn, and knew that if she didn't act quickly, two things would happen. Peter would play football and Hailey would flirt shamelessly. Again. *Time to nip this in the bud.*

You may sit with your mama, but if I see you acting up, there'll be the piper to pay."

"What's dat mean?" Kaylee stared wide-eyed.

"If you are naughty, there'll be a punishment when we get back home."

"I don't want dat." A tear rolled down her cheek.

"It's okay, Honey. I know that you'll be an incredibly good girl.

Okay. Let's go. Remember, I'm watching you."

Kaylee is such a sweet and sensitive girl. I hate having to use the sledgehammer when she's around, but sometimes a mama's got to do what a mama's got to do.

~

Betsy came running towards her children as fast as her spindly little legs would allow.

"My babies! How I've missed you!" She knelt and smothered Kaylee and Jenny in kisses and hugs.

Hailey rolled her eyes, and Peter squirmed away, while Jenny stood her ground bravely, and Kaylee giggled with glee. "Mama! We missed ya so much!"

"And I missed all ya'll!"

Mrs. Baker took a step back away from the Freeman children to give them a little privacy. Betsy looked up at her and met her eyes. "They look good. You've got to tell me what you're feeding them and what you've managed to do with Kaylee's hair. I cudn't never get that right."

Mrs. Baker smiled. "Sure, Betsy. I would love to

catch up. You down for coffee sometime?"

"I'm more of a tea drinker. There's a doughnut shop downtown. It'd be fun ta go dere."

~

On Monday when the Freeman children went back to school, Peter's old gang met him at his locker. "Well, here he comes, guys. His dad's a drunken jailbird." They guffawed as he opened his locker and all his books fell out in a heap. Peter balled up his fists and stared at them. Because of Mrs. Baker's rules, he knew that he should not fight, but they didn't know that. Otherwise, he'd wipe the smiles right off their faces.

From the first homeroom bell until the next class, Peter and Jenny's classmates taunted them mercilessly. It did not feel so good for the Freeman bullies to get a taste of their own medicine. Their unkindness had come full circle. At lunchtime, Peter yelled at them, "Leave us alone!"

"Whatcha gonna do about it, huh?" The leader stared him down.

Finally, they had enough. Mrs. Baker's rules or not, this turning the other cheek business was for the birds. Peter nodded, and Jenny knew what to do. She took off running headlong into the leader, knocking him off his feet before he had a chance to object.

Peter entered the fray with fists swinging left and right. The bullies ran off holding their bloodied noses. He dusted his hands together and scowled. He knew better than to be mean, but he didn't care.

Their poor choices landed them in the Principal's Office.

"I'm disappointed in you, Peter, and Jenny. You have been so well-behaved the last few weeks. What happened?"

They hung their heads. Peter mumbled, "They wouldn't leave us alone, so we made 'em."

"Well, the law says I must send a report to Children's Services."

Peter shrugged. "Go ahead. See if'n I care."

Jenny added her two cents. "So, what else cud we do? Da teachers wudn't do nothin' bout it. Dey saw it happenin' ta us and turned dere heads away. What kind of adult does dat? Dey're s'posed to look out for us kids."

Mrs. Baker showed up to take them home. They silently gathered their things and marched to her van. Before she started the vehicle, she turned to them. "Now, Peter and Jenny, you broke the rules by what you did, so there must be consequences. The two of you will stay home from school tomorrow as a suspension punishment. Don't think this will be a picnic. Both of you chose to do wrong. You had better options but didn't take them. So, I have the assignments from your teachers. Both of you will complete those right after breakfast. I will be checking your work. If it is sloppy, or less than your best effort, we will sit at this table and get it right. Then you will write a letter to Principal White apologizing for your attitude. Do I make myself clear?"

"Yes, ma'am."

"No more fighting." She pulled into the garage and turned to the children again. "Since you have the energy to fight, your same vigor can be for beneficial use. I've made up a list of special chores for you to do. There will be no electronics today. And to one up that, I won't serve dessert if the chore list remains by suppertime.

"Peter, you can start by taking a scrub brush and bucket of warm soapy water and clean every inch of the deck. Then, the garage needs swept out.

"Jenny, you'll be polishing all the silverware, and every faucet in the kitchen and bathrooms. They need to shine like a mirror.

"I will keep an eye on your progress. My dad always told me to inspect what I expect. And that's exactly what I will do. Your job is to do your chores right with a good attitude."

Peter and Jenny hung their heads and scowled as they climbed out of the van and stomped toward the house.

"Umm. Attitude check. Get your heads up and take the punishments like a young gentleman and lady should." Mrs. Baker reminded them.

15 News

Dear Mama: I got some big news. I had ta go before a judge again for a review of my case. Da guards told him dat I ain't been causin' any trouble, so da judge looked at me and said, "Good job, Freeman. Dat's what I wanna hear." He glanced at a bunch of papers, and shuffled dem around a bit. He cleared da big hawker outta his throat den said, "Because of yer record, I am gonna let ya out in thirty days. Ya won't be servin' da whole sentence." I wanted ta jump up and down, but I had to keep my cool.

I'm gonna be on probation for a year, den, gotta go ta a special school for kids like me. I think it's called alternative education for youth offenders. Dat's nothin'. I learned my lesson. I ain't dealing no more drugs. Bobby or no Bobby! Don't need ta mess up my life for no amount of money. It was a dumb idea and da police caught me red-handed. Da hurtful stuff I done is in da past. God erased my record. Now, I must get people ta trust me again dat I won't do dis again. I got memories of da kids in school overdosin' on some of da stuff I sold dem. I didn't care what happened ta dem, but now dat I had time ta think about it, I feel sick ta my stomach. Some of da kids didn't make it. Dat haunts me. I cud blame myself, but Jesus forgave me, and He is helping me ta do better. I wrote an apology letter ta every family dat had a kid dat took da weed dat I sold. I got a bunch back sayin' dat dey forgive me. Some were mean and wanna press charges, but I'm not worried. God will take care of me. I'm doin' so much better.

I got ta thinkin' dat I need ta get a proper job when I get out. I wanna save up money ta buy a car and put some aside for school things. Don't know if'n I'll go to college or not. I'll know better when da time comes.

I want ta help ya with da money problems at home too. I know Dad's s'posed ta provide for his family, but he ain't gonna be able ta do dat for a while. As da oldest son, I got da responsibility ta step up ta da plate and give ya a hand.

I've been prayin' about dat kind of stuff. God will help us cuz I asked Him to.

He's already helpin' me with da forgiveness thing too. I got another chance. Dad should too.

Pastor J told me dat Dad has been workin' at clean-up duty at home for a few hours a day. He picks up rocks and hauls dirt and sand for the crew buildin' da basement.

Da judge didn't want him sittin' round feelin' sorry for himself. He may be weak, but da demanding work keeps his mind active so he ain't thinkin' bout da booze. Dat's a good thing, don't ya think? Gives me hope dat he'll come home better cuz he had a part in rebuildin' da house dat fell apart. He's startin' ta do da right thing.

I pray for him every day, and for ya and da rest of da family. We're gonna do better when we're all together again.

I can't wait to see you.
Love, Joseph.

~

Dear Joseph: Ya make my heart happy. I'm so proud of ya for comin' such a long way from da boy ya were. God way up dere in da sky is helpin' ya so much. Yer attitude is so good. I'm readin' da pages of a boy who's become a young man...a good one at dat. Yer gettin' so kind and good. God way up in da sky is changin' ya.

I got news too. Hailey's with Mrs. Baker now. Dat woman done worked a miracle with da kids. Dey sit at da table sayin' 'scuse me and thank ya. Dey don't act like dey did. After Dad's hearin' we went ta Pizza Palace. Da food was so good! Hailey got sick and had ta be in da hospital again. Dey say she's gonna have migraine headaches da rest of her life. Kinda makes me mad all over again ta think bout it. She was brave , but Peter was too. Ya kids are makin' me proud enough ta bust a button or two.

I'm so glad dat Dad is workin' with da crew re-buildin' da house. Hope it helps him think better thoughts and not want da liquid fire anymore.

Our lives are changin' ,and I'm happy bout it. Keep doin' good, son.

Love, Mama

16 Changes

Thomas arrived at Brock's Home directly from the Sober Living Program. He threw his knapsack in the corner and plopped down on his bed. Sleep came swiftly. It seemed like a few minutes, but he slept for several hours. It was now morning, and the incessant pounding on his door pulled him out of his dreaming.

Dis is as bad as a jail. No sleep for da weary.

He dragged his achy body to the door. "Yeah. Whaddya want?"

"Good morning, Thomas. Breakfast is in 15 minutes."

"Yeah, Yeah, okay." Thomas slammed the door, yawned, and looked at the clock. 6:00 A.M.

He dug through his bag and found a tee shirt and jogging pants. *Guess dese'll do.*

He opened his door and walked to the end of the hall, then followed the symbols on the signs until he found the dining room. He warily looked around. *Dere's lotsa guys just like me. Maybe dis won't be so bad.*

"Come join us." Some men waved Thomas toward

an empty chair. "You must be the fellow who came from Riftwood late last night."

"I'm Thomas Freeman." He yawned widely and covered his mouth to hide his serious need for dental care.

The men introduced themselves. Some wore suits and ties; others had work uniforms on. *Ev'rybody's goin ta work 'cept me. I wanna go back ta bed!*

Soon, the breakfast line formed, and the men from his table joined the others. Thomas salivated as he saw men with trays of delicious food walk by. *Ain't never seen did much fodder in my life. Lots better lookin' dan da detox or jail slop!* Finally, it was his turn. Ham and scrambled eggs, pancakes, sausages, bread pudding, bagels, and all kinds of fruit. *If I hang round dis place very long, I'm gonna be as big as da neighbor's bull.*

Back at the table, a man named Todd piped up, "Soon, you'll join us going out to work."

Thomas interrupted him. "Who's ta say I ain't been workin'? Da judge made me do clean up duty on my property, so dey cud build another house for da family."

"That's a wonderful way to show them how much you care about them."

Thomas shrugged. "Judge Paxton said it'd build character in me. I ain't seen any changes. Da only thing I got is cuts, scrapes, and scars to prove dat I was out dere workin' like a crazy man. But my missus and da kids will be happy livin' in a new place while I have nine months here away from ev'rybody."

"Ya need some cupcakes for your pity party, man? No sense complaining. Everybody here has struggled just like you. Mr. Harrington and the staff can help you to mend fences from your past. You'll walk out of here with your head held high and a spring in your step. Thomas, you can do this. We're proof that changes happen.

"Some of us will be going back to our families soon. Hang in there because time will fly by and before you know it, your turn will come."

"Yeah, right. My Betsy put a year of no contact on me, so I'll be here a while."

"That bad, huh? My wife did the same thing to me."

"Really?"

"Yep."

"You'll get through this. It's hard at first but you'll find a routine. We'll all be here to help you."

"Thanks for dat." Thomas yawned again and hid his rotted teeth.

"You'll adjust to living here. See you when we get back." They all stood, pushed in their chairs, emptied their trays, then headed out the double doors.

After they left, Thomas sat alone at the table for a few minutes taking in what they said.

Shortly, a well-dressed man approached and sat down across from him. "I'm Ed Harrington." He stuck out his hand to shake with Thomas. "Welcome to Brock's Home. I see you met some of our other men at the breakfast table. If you listen to their stories, you can find some similarities.

"But that's enough of that. We offer services to help each man become successful in everything he does."

"I got lots of mess-ups with my life."

"Brock's Home is a place of second and third

chances."

"I need dat."

"We start with your education background. Did you graduate from High School?"

"Nah. "I ain't very good at school." Thomas stuttered. "I had ta leave when I was sixteen cuz Grandpappy died. Granny needed me to stay home and help her."

Ed wrote something on his clipboard. "Our first goal will be to enter you into GED classes. Tutors will work with you to help you pass your exams. What do you think about that?"

"I got a hard time readin'," Thomas admitted.

"Our next goal will be to help you learn to read better. Why don't we go to the classroom?" They both stood and pushed in their chairs.

~

A dark-haired man with glasses sat at a large mahogany desk across the room. *Clickety-clack!* Several men tapped on keyboards at small stations. As they approached, the man looked up and stood. "Hello. I'm Professor Broadman." He shook hands with both men.

Mr. Harrington shared Thomas's details.

"Very well, I will take it from here."

Professor Broadman led Thomas to a small desk and pulled a chair up beside him. "I understand that you have problems with reading." He tapped a few keys on the computer, then printed off a page of large font text for Thomas. It was not easy, but he got every word correct.

"Very good, Thomas, let us try another page."

This time the font was smaller, and he squinted.

The letters blurred and ran into each other. Thomas took a deep breath and willed his eyes to cooperate, but they refused to focus. He stumbled over most of the words. "It's okay, Thomas. We will try something else." Professor Broadman laid a page of simple addition and subtraction in front of him.

"The numbers are too small." Thomas was squinting again.

"Okay. Your eyes need to be examined. People can struggle with reading if they can't see the printed page in front of them. Come." He motioned for Thomas to follow.

Professor Broadman led him to an elevator, up to the next level, and down a long hall. Thomas squinted and tried hard to make out the letters on the door. They entered and walked up to the receptionist. "Thomas needs his eyes checked." Professor Broadman sat down in the waiting area while Thomas and the ophthalmologist entered a large room.

"Wow! Dere's a lot of machines in here. I never had da eyes checked. Will it hurt?"

Doctor Townsend led Thomas to the examining chair. "Not at all. Once you settle into the chair, we will begin."

The eye doctor explained everything that he was doing. After the exam, he put drops in Thomas's eyes. "I need to make sure they are healthy. If not, hopefully we can make them better."

Within a short while, nothing was clear. Finally, Thomas sat down in the chair again, and Doctor Townsend shone a flashlight in his eyes. The ophthalmologist shut it off and flipped on the overhead lights. He sat at his desk and wrote on a notepad. "You need reading glasses, Thomas. Take this next door and they will help you pick out a pair of glasses."

Afterward, Professor Broadman took him to his room. "You need to rest now. We will try again tomorrow after breakfast." Thomas lay down on his bed exhausted from his morning. His head throbbed.

At lunchtime, Mr. Harrington brought a tray to him and sat down on Thomas's bed while he ate at a small desk. "Do you have a family, Thomas?"

"Yep. Got a wife, Betsy, and five kids from four to fifteen years old."

"You can call them at night if you wish."

"Nope. Got nine more months of a no contact order. I'm countin' down da days." Thomas took another bite of his hamburger. "I miss dem like crazy."

"It's okay. I'll get you a notebook, so you can write down your letters to your family. You don't have to mail them, but it will help you feel less anxious.

"I hope I can stay away from drinkin'. Da judge said I'd go to prison if I drink one drop of alcohol. I gotta get enrolled in AA yet. Dat's part of da sentence."

"Okay. There's a meeting in the All-Purpose room tonight at six o'clock. I'll introduce you to the leader at supper."

Thomas went back to dreamland until another knock awakened him.

"Supper in fifteen minutes."

He remembered to make himself as presentable as possible, then headed to the dining hall with his growling stomach.

He sat down at the table with the same men he had talked to at breakfast. When it was time to serve the meal, they rushed to form a line. Everybody was hungry.

When Thomas sat down at the table again, Todd informed him. "After supper, we all do our part to clean up. It's part of living here. Afterward, we have some fun outside. Tonight's game is softball. Have you played it before?"

"Yeah. A long time ago."

"What was your favorite position?"

"Third base."

"You've got it. Let's go."

"Umm, I can't play. I have an AA meeting tonight at six."

"That's okay. If you get done in time, please join us."

The meeting was over by 6:30 P.M., so Thomas went outside to cheer on the other men. He taunted in playful fun. "Hey niner, niner, niner, Hey niner, niner. Get a hit, get a hit, get a hit. Niner, niner, niner, Get a hit!"

CRACK! The batter connected with the ball and hit it over the fence.

"Home Run!" yelled Thomas as three runners slid into home base.

They all whooped and hollered. It didn't matter who won, everybody joined in to celebrate a great game.

They did not need alcohol to have fun. I miss playin' games like dis. Thomas thought.

That night Thomas sat on the edge of his bed and opened to the first page of his notebook. `Dear Betsy: I'm thinkin' bout ya so much...`

He put his head down and wept as he remembered what put this separation between him and his wife. He closed the notebook on his tear-stained pages. *"God, how can I fix da mess I'm in?"*

I'll help you with each step. Rest now."

That night, Thomas slept like a baby.

17   The   List

Caroline looked up the number for Children's Services and dialed Felicity's extension from the main menu. *Please, God, help me find a way to connect to Thomas's family.*

"Hello," Felicity growled with a mouthful of food.

"I saw you at the sentencing hearing for my son, Thomas Freeman. I didn't know that he had a family. I want to make up for lost time. They need me as much as I need them."

"Why are you calling me?" Felicity huffed.

"Grandparent rights." *Two could play this game.*

"I see." Felicity scratched her head. "Hmm." She flipped through her schedule. "Come see me today at 3PM. If everything checks out, then I'll ask the judge to grant permission for you.

"It will take a few weeks for the results of fingerprints, a background check, and credit history."

"That shouldn't be a problem. I'm a 911 dispatcher. I just updated those documents last month. I'll call the secretary and have her fax the information to you." Caroline hit the red button on her phone. *She didn't scare me with her gruffness. I deal with that every day. Those kids need a grandma, and I'm going to fight for as long as it takes. You're not stopping me from seeing them.*

~

After Felicity hung up, she thought. *If that woman thinks she's gonna step in here and claim them after all these years, she has another thought coming. If she doesn't show the proof, I'll stop her for the fraud that she is. Even if she is their grandmother, she must prove it.*

~

Caroline arrived promptly at 3:00 P.M. in her work uniform. "Did you receive the fax?"

"Yes, it looks like everything is in order." Felicity shuffled the paperwork and clipped them together in a file named, "Freeman." "Remember, they don't know you, so I'll set up a fifteen-minute session for you in a few weeks. What time works best for you?"

"I need to be at work at 3:30 P.M."

"Okey-dokey," Felicity said as she shut her laptop case.

A few weeks later, a woman entered the Children's Services Office with four youngsters. After making Mrs. Baker comfortable in the waiting area, Felicity brought the children back to the conference room to meet Caroline.

"Are ya my grandma? Are ya a cop? I'm scared of dem." Kaylee stuck her thumb in her mouth.

"No. I answer the phone for people who are sick or in trouble. I send help for them when they need it. To answer your first question; I am your daddy's mama, so that makes me your grandma."

"I like ya." Kaylee sat down next to her at the

table.

"How come we ain't seen ya before?" Jenny interrupted.

"I live about ten miles away; and I never knew about you all. It's time to change that. Next is Jenny, right?"

"How'd ya know my name?"

"I was at the sentencing hearing for your daddy, remember?"

Jenny nodded.

"And you are Peter." Caroline tried to make conversation with him, but he just scowled.

Just like his daddy. He puts on a tough exterior, but underneath, he's a scared little boy.

Caroline turned to the only child left at the table. "Hailey?"

She nodded and smiled.

This girl really needs someone in her life that can be there for her no matter what.

Caroline stood, went around the table, and hugged her.

"It'll be cool to have a grandma," Hailey smiled.

"I can't wait to visit with all of you later, but I have to go to work now." Caroline waved goodbye to them.

~

Felicity went to visit Betsy. When she came downstairs all out of breath, she blurted, "Is dere somethin' wrong?" Betsy nervously chewed her fingernails.

"No." Felicity opened a folder and laid it on the table for her to follow along.

"What's all dis?" Betsy stared wide-eyed.

"There's a process you have to follow to be reunited with your children."

"Dere my kids and a bunch of peoples is buildin' us a new house. So, what's da problem?"

"New house or not, we can't allow them to live with you until these conditions are met."

"Is dat so?" Betsy put on her warrior maiden stance, but Felicity ignored her.

"For example, we need to know if you can support your family once you are all together again. You don't have a husband to help with them."

"Who'd ya think took care of dem when he was 'round? It wasn't him; I tell ya for sure and certain. Dat lazy slob did nothin' but tip da bottle and beat us up."

"The rules say that a parent must be employed full-time. Have you found a new job yet?"

"No, but I've been down ta da Employment Office and dere helpin' me ta get applications and da resume` thingy done, but I'm havin' trouble."

"What's wrong?" Felicity queried.

"I don't got any references. You're s'posed ta have two people say good things about ya, so dey can make ya look good to da hirer man. Where I worked before won't bring me back cuz dey hated me, and I liked dem as much as a toothache."

"I see," Felicity replied. "That does present a problem. Have you talked to Deborah? She might put in a good word for you."

"I'll ask her. What's next on your list?" Betsy scratched the idea on a napkin.

"You have to pass two drug tests."

"No problem. Give me a cup, and I'll go pee in it."

"It's not that easy. You must schedule an

appointment with one of two drug testing centers."

"So, I gotta schedule peein' in a cup? Dat's dumb."

"I don't make the rules, I just tell you what has to be done." Felicity stifled a chuckle to remain professional.

"It's gonna be tough." Betsy sighed. "What if I can't do it all?"

"The judge needs to see a 'good-faith effort' on your case plan to bring the children back home from foster care."

"I'm doin' my best. What else do ya 'spect?"

"Make sure to keep good records of your progress, so the judge can see what you're doing. The last page is a list of parenting classes that you'll need to complete."

Wait. What? I gotta go ta school? Was never good at it. Wonder if I'm gonna write on da blackboard and do homework. It's been so long... Betsy's mind took her down a bunny trail of thorns and thistles. *Da other kids picked on me somethin' awful cuz of my red hair.* She shivered hoping it would not be like that.

Felicity kept blabbering on about her contingency plan, whatever that was.

"Is dat all? My brain's fried ta a crisp like a slab of crunchy smoked bacon." Betsy sighed deeply. "I'm gonna have ta burn da candle at both ends ta make dis happen."

Felicity handed her a card. "Please call if you have any questions, I'll help you in any way I can as long as you cooperate."

When she left, Betsy sat there dazed. *What in da world am I gonna do?* She bowed her head and prayed, *God, way up dere in da sky, I don't know what ta do. Cud ya help me?* As she waited for an answer, her eyes were drawn to Caroline's number. It was like a bright light turned on in her head. *I know.*

Betsy dialed her number. "Can we meet?"

"Sure, why?"

"I got dis problem. Da big-headed Felicity showed up with a looong list of things I gotta do. My brain's goin' fifty miles ta nowhere."

"I see. Why don't we meet tomorrow for lunch at Burger Joint?"

Betsy smiled. "Dat's finer dan frog's hair."

At high noon Betsy pulled up to Burger Joint with her "List."

Once they ordered and gobbled down their food, she blurted. "I've been tryin' ta get a job, but ain't nobody wantin' ta hire me." Betsy sighed.

Caroline suddenly stood up and grabbed her tray. "I've got it! Why don't we try the bakery on Fourth Street? I saw a "Help Wanted" sign in the window yesterday. Let's go."

"Are ya serious? I love ta bake and make food purty. I did it at da diner all da time."

Betsy opened the door and marched up to the front counter. "Ya'll are hirin,' and I need a job. What do I have ta do?"

The cashier handed her an application. Betsy's fingers fumbled with the pen as she filled in all the blanks.

"Do you have a resume' to add to it?" Caroline inquired.

"Yeah," Betsy pulled a neatly typed one out of her voluminous purse and returned to the counter.

"Here ya go." She handed the papers to the clerk.

"Have a seat while I take this to the manager." The cashier turned and went through double doors, then quickly approached the table with a man in a flour-dusted apron.

When they completed the interview, they stood, shook hands, and Betsy turned smiling from ear to ear.

Once outside the store, Betsy bubbled over with excitement, "I got a job working from 4 A.M. until 11 A.M. Next is ta figure out who can stay with da kids in da morning ta get dem ta da school bus."

"Well, I get off at 3:30 A.M. I drive on Highway 721 right past your house on the way home. I'll stop in and get the older ones on the bus, then, I'll take Kaylee to daycare. We will get through this together as a family."

"I like dat, family." Betsy waved goodbye to her.

18 Thomas Can Read.

The long months of no contact wore heavily on his mind, but Thomas felt hopeful about eventually hearing from his family. Now, he needed to practice reading. He went to the classroom and Professor Broadman helped him choose a simplistic book. "Here, use these magnification glasses until your own are ready."

Thomas sat down in a comfortable chair in the corner, put the glasses on, and opened his book. The letters showed themselves boldly and clearly. As he read aloud quietly to himself, his confidence grew. Each word became a steppingstone to the next one. Sometimes he sat for a moment trying to figure the longer words out. Then, suddenly, they began to make sense. He finished his first book in no time and rushed to find Professor Broadman.

"Congratulations, Thomas. I knew you could do it." He handed him another book.

"Do ya have a Bible I cud learn ta read?"

"Of course, Here is the audio version to follow along with it."

"Thank ya." Thomas raced upstairs to put the Bible

CDs and player in his top drawer. He started heading out of his room again when Mr. Harrington stopped him. "How are you doing?"

"Great. I read a book by myself." Thomas proudly announced.

"That's wonderful news. Way to go!" He patted Thomas on the shoulder.

"The reason I came up here, was to ask if you would like to have your hair trimmed today. There's an opening right now at the barbershop."

"I reckon dat dis sheep needs sheared bad. Let's do dis." Thomas closed his door, and they headed downstairs, and around the block.

Thomas leaned back in the chair as Barber Jack massaged his scalp and washed his hair. Then, *Snip! Buzz! Whoosh!* Lots of hair fell to the floor as the groomer worked. When he spun him around, he asked, "What do you think, Thomas?"

"Wow! I can't believe it's me." Thomas admired himself in the mirror.

Mr. Harrington paid the bill, then they walked back to Brock's Home. Instead of slumping along, Thomas walked with his head held high.

When they got back home, Professor Broadman waited with a math test for him to try. Thomas put the magnification glasses on, and easily answered as many as he could until he reached the algebra section. Then, he bogged down and guessed. When he was through, he took the test to Professor Broadman.

After a delicious lunch, Mr. Harrington met with Thomas again. This time they talked about what he liked to do.

"I don't got no hobbies cuz all I did was drink and

deal with hangovers."

"If you could do anything, what would it be?"

"I loved ta plant things an' see dem pop through da dirt. Granny always told me I had a green thumb."

"Maybe you could go back to farming."

"Nah. Dat don't leave time for a family. Ya gotta get up early, tend da animals, den work til dark and do it all over 'gain."

"There are various kinds of farming. What if you were to grow wheat and corn but not have animals? Would that be easier?"

"Too much risk. Ya get a hard rain and yer done for."

"What about if you had a tree and plant nursery on your farm?"

"I'd like that."

"We have a greenhouse out back which provides food for the table, and some left over to sell at the local farmers' market. Would you like to try that?"

Thomas's eyes glowed with delight. "When can I start?"

"Soon. I'll work on the details, and let you know."

The lunch bell rang, and Thomas raced to get into line.

Where had the morning gone?

19 Joseph

On Friday, his last day in juvie, Joseph sat on the edge of his bunk bed, then stood and paced his cell. He looked through the bars and saw the guards with the cafeteria cart slowly making their way around the corridors. His stomach rumbled, but he knew that the food would taste like it came out of a dumpster. "Lunch. Stand back!" The guard shoved in the tray.

Eww! It's disgustin', but I need to eat somethin'. Joseph plugged his nose and drank the thin soup quickly. The lingering oil nearly made him spew it out of his mouth like the whale spit up Jonah. He munched on the dry hunk of toast, and it took the taste away.

Can't wait ta get a decent meal. I've been starvin' since da cops dragged me in here. Good thing Pastor J brings me candy bars. Dey keep me alive.

Joseph folded his blanket and placed the pillow on top of it. His personal belongings were arranged in the issued box from the guards. Everything was in order.

Before he knew it, the guards unlocked his cell. "Let's go, Freeman, today you get to blow this popsicle stand. But, if we see you here again, you'll be like a cat at a dog convention." One guard poked him in the chest to emphasize it.

"Yes sir."

By then, they had reached the Release Officer. The guards unfastened the cuffs and restored his belongings. "Good luck." The heavy metal doors and deafening buzzer sounded as they retreated inside.

Joseph slipped into the restroom and dropped the county owned property in the hamper. *Ahh! Street clothes again. Dey sag a bit, but dere better dan da hot itchy uniform.*

"Get outta here and don't come back." The officer unlocked the door.

Yay! No more juvie for me. I'm done with it!

On the other side stood Pastor Johnson. "Am I ever glad to see ya," Joseph raced to him and gave him a bear hug.

"Are you ready?" The minister opened the outside door.

"Ya kiddin'? I spent six months in dat place and wanna get as far away as I can."

"So why are we just sauntering along?"

"Is dat a challenge?"

"Yes."

Joseph took off running like a scalded rabbit toward a car that flashed its lights and honked its horn.

"Dat red car yours?" Joseph looked over his shoulder at the pastor who struggled to catch him. "I thought ya'd be

drivin' a Cadillac instead of dis match box."

"Hey, now. You are dissing my car."

"Nah, I like little run-abouts." Joseph stopped at the passenger's side of the Ford Focus and climbed in.

Once he fastened his seatbelt, he turned to the pastor. "Thanks for givin' me a ride."

"No problem, buddy. Glad to do it."

Before Pastor Johnson started the engine, he explained to Joseph, "You won't be going home yet, because your mama is finishing the red tape with Children's Social Services."

"I miss her," Joseph frowned. "I hoped we cud be together."

"I know, but Mrs. Baker has an opening, so you'll live with your siblings. We are going to surprise your mama on Sunday."

"Dat wud be kinda cool."

When they pulled up to Mrs. Baker's house, Joseph said, "At least I'll be with my brother and sisters. I'm kinda nervous."

"Ah, don't be. They're excited to see you." Pastor Johnson put the car in gear, then reached over the seat, and grabbed a grocery bag. "Comfort food." He chuckled.

"Ya remembered." Joseph ripped the bag open. "Here ya go," he offered one to the pastor. "Glad ya like dese. Other people don't know what dey're missin'." He fist-bumped him.

They opened their car doors and slammed them in unison. Pastor Johnson grabbed a suitcase from the trunk. Joseph stared at him.

"You need clean underclothes and jeans, right? The caseworker gave them to me because she had to be out of town at a convention today."

Joseph nodded, appreciative of his thoughtful friend.

"You'll meet with Felicity in the morning."

"What do ya mean?" Joseph puzzled that thought for a moment.

"You'll understand more tomorrow. Until that time, try to behave."

"I promise. Can't be as bad as juvie."

His siblings raced to him to get a group hug. He picked up Kaylee and whirled her around. "See, told ya I'd be back soon." She snuggled in a little closer.

Mrs. Baker led him inside.

"Come on," Peter, his little brother, impatiently tugged on his sleeve. "Dis is da boys' room, and down da hall ta da left is da bathroom. Here's your bed. I claimed da top bunk already, so ya get da bottom."

"I don't mind. Anythin' is better dan juvie."

Joseph Dutch-rubbed him. "Yer gettin' so tall. What happened ta da li'l squirt dat I left behind?"

"Duh. I grew." Peter laughed. "I'm so happy ya can be here with us."

"Me too." Joseph opened his suitcase and put his clothes away.

Soon a little bell sounded.

"What's dat for?" Joseph looked around.

"It means dat we must scrub up for supper. I'll race ya ta da bathroom." Peter took off like greased lightning.

~

The next morning Felicity, Pastor Johnson, and his Probation Officer, visited with Joseph and Mrs. Baker at length to spell out their expectations.

"Joseph, until the final paperwork is in place, you will remain in Mrs. Baker's care except when visits with your mother are arranged."

"K." Joseph turned and looked out the window.

Bein' a short-term placement isn't dat bad. No bangin' doors, screamin' guards, or cryin' in da night.... And da food here is a world better dan the slop dey fed us at da Juvie Center. I'm gonna do all right.

20 Welcome Home, Betsy

The list from Children's Social Services was wrinkled and dog-eared. Betsy whipped it out daily. "I'm gettin' dere," she told Felicity on her next visit. "I'm workin' as hard as I can to get da kids back. Dey're more important dan anythin' in da world."

~

When the County Housing Inspector handed her the keys to her house, Betsy was elbow-deep in bread dough, but danced a little waist down jig. *It's a long time comin', but now I can move in. I don't care if I have ta sleep on da floor for a while. It's my house!*

Betsy couldn't wait to get off work. She raced back to the women's shelter and packed her bags.

"Hey, whatcha' doin'?" One of the ladies asked.

"I'm goin' home."

"As in what? Back to the man who beat ya to a pulp. Dat ain't home, honey, dat's prison."

"My husband's been in detox, and he's got several months left on his no contact order."

"How long do ya think that'll stick before he's

back to beatin' ya like a punchin' dummy."

Betsy sighed. "Thanks for rainin' on my parade. He ain't comin' back for a while. I'll be ramblin' around in da house by my lonesome...at least until da kids come back."

"If he slaps ya again, ya make quick comin' back down here. We'll take care of him good and proper."

Betsy gathered her things and hugged her roommates goodbye. *I'm gonna miss my friends at da shelter. Hope I'll see dem again someday.*

Tears streamed down Betsy's face as she backed out of her parking spot. Her friends stood on the front porch waving to her as she pulled away. *Dey're like da sisters I never had. I learned so much from dem. Dey're my forever friends.*

Soon, she arrived at the farm. The hairs on the back of Betsy's neck stood straight up. She cautiously walked to the door looking all around. *Wonder if someone is in da house. I didn't come dis far ta let a loser hurt me, but I ain't takin' a chance.* Her friends' warnings echoed in her ears as she raced back to her car and locked the doors. Then, Betsy slumped down in the seat out of sight of anyone who might be lurking.

She picked up her phone and called Deborah Johnson. "I'm sittin' at da farm, shakin' like a bowl of Jello®. What if somebody's in dere?"

"It's okay, Betsy. I'm here for you. Do you need me to stay on the line?"

"Yeah. Dis ain't such an easy thing."

"You've done hard stuff before. I'm so proud of the amazing strong woman that you've become. You got this."

"Can we pray before I get back out of da car?"

"Sure."

"Father in Heaven, be with Betsy right now. You know that she's scared to step into this new chapter of her life. Keep her safe from harm and give her the strength to take each step toward the house unafraid because your angels cover her on the left, right, above, and beside her."

"Amen." Betsy shouted into the phone.

She thrust open and slammed the car door shut, marched toward the house, head up high, and shoulders back. She held her key like a mini nine-millimeter. This time she put it in the lock and flung it wide open. She shouted into the empty house. "My name is Betsy Freeman and I'm not afraid anymore. This is MY house. I'm here to stay. Anybody else better git out before I give ya a reason to run."

One could see that the old Betsy Freeman was back in style…the mighty, the loud, the strong warrior.

~

Early Saturday morning, two burly men made their way to the truck rental business. "Dis da one, Charlie?"

"Yep, Ron. It's da biggest on da lot. Let's get da keys and head on outta here." The men swaggered inside. "We're here ta pick up da truck for da Community Church."

"Right. The preacher already paid for it." The cashier slid the keys across the counter. "Bring 'er back in one piece, guys." He grinned. "Help yourselves to some wake-up coffee." He pointed to the far corner of the room.

"Ya don't have to tell us twice."

The moving van lumbered out of the parking lot and down Prospect Street. "Traffic's light, so why did we come to a standstill? I wonder what happened." Charlie took a sip of the scalding dark brew.

"I see the flashing lights around the corner," Ron replies as he lifted his cup to his lips. "Looks kinda bad from here."

"At least we can sit here and enjoy our coffee while we wait."

Finally, the moving van began to inch its way along again. "Must have been a bunch of rubberneckers ahead of us." Ron glanced at the wreckage alongside the road. "It looks like a hopped-up sports car met the semi on the turn.

From the skid marks, I'd say that the car was at fault. I wonder if there are fatalities." Ron took another sip of his coffee.

"I'd say the car didn't stand a chance for survivors, but you never know." Charlie downshifted to round the corner of the church's street.

~

Meanwhile, a group of men waited to load the community's donations bound for the Freeman Farm. Martin Clark looked at his watch. "They're fifteen minutes late. What's holding them up?"

"I don't know," Pastor Johnson replied. *Surely nothing would happen today after all the Freeman family has been through.* He shook his head, not allowing his mind to go there.

Shortly, the moving van pulled around the corner and stopped at the side of the church. Charlie and Ron jumped out, drew the ramp down, and shoved the back door up.

"Okay guys, load 'er up."

"About time you lazy goons got here," Frederick

Howard teased.

Charlie pulled himself to his full height, stomped over, and got in his face. "Who are ya callin' lazy, huh? For your info, we were outta bed long before the sun turned the sky pink. So, who's lazy now?" He smirked.

"What took you so long?" Frederick prodded.

"A sports car met a semi on a curve, and it didn't turn out so good."

"You don't say."

"Yeah."

"Hey, you two, stop jawin'. Dis truck ain't loadin' itself." A volunteer called as he and a helper struggled up the ramp with the first piece of furniture.

"See, yer jabberin' got us both in trouble. Now whaddya got ta say?"

"Nothing." Frederick hopped up onto the ramp to lend a hand.

With a shove here and a groan there, Charlie walked up the incline, pulled the back door into place on the loaded truck, then hopped in the driver's seat. Soon, a plume of diesel smoke clouded the air as the moving van slowly crept through the streets and out of town.

~

Meanwhile, at the Freeman Farm, the bakery van off-loaded trays of mouth-watering goodies. "We made dose yesterday," Betsy stuck out her chest. "Da bake shop makes lotsa good stuff every day."

Quick as you could say, Jack Spratt, the delicious treats lay in an orderly fashion on the tables, and the bakery's van headed back to town.

Soon, Betsy heard the moving truck's lower gear grind as it turned into the driveway and crept up the hill like an elephant pulling a passenger train. Once Charlie jockeyed it in position, he and Ron jumped out and unlocked the back.

"We're starved." Charlie declared as he swaggered over to the tables.

Once the volunteers polished off mountains of goodies, the men were like a bunch of worker ants crawling all over the house with their deposits of furniture and boxes.

~

Betsy darted like a dragonfly, back and forth. "Put dat here, no, dere. Dose go over dere." One would think she was a professional interior designer. The colors and furniture coordinated beautifully as her house developed into a stunning masterpiece.

"We'll see ya at lunch," Charlie called to Betsy as the truck lurched forward and inched its way down the driveway.

I bet ya will. Men! Always wantin' somethin' ta eat when dere's work ta do.

At noon, Mrs. Hudson, Hailey's former algebra teacher, arrived.

Betsy raced to greet her. "Hi! Whatcha doin' here?"

"We brought lunch."

"That is so nice of ya. How can we pay ya back?"

"Pshaw! You don't owe anything. It's the least we can do to help your family on its big day. Where do you want the food to be set up?"

"Right over dere." Betsy pointed to the tables beside the house.

Turning to her crew, Mrs. Hudson motioned to

them. "Let's go, guys. We've got a hungry crowd to feed."

Betsy turned to look down the driveway as the moving van squeaked its way up it. Creaky springs complaining like old men's knees, the cab and box rolling dramatically back and forth over the muddy ruts.

Perfect timing, Betsy chuckled.

Everybody rushed to the lunch table like buffaloes on a stampede.

As Mrs. Hudson and her crew loaded the empty pans back into her van, Betsy side-arm hugged her. "Thanks for doin' dat. It made people happy."

"It is our pleasure." Mrs. Hudson closed the back doors and jumped into the driver's seat.

After lunch, Mrs. Baker arrived with the kiddos who raced up the stairs. "They've been dying to see their new house. I hope you didn't mind my bringing them here."

"No problem. Thanks for doin' dat. I miss dem."

"I'm glad to be there for them as long as they need."

She has no idea. I only have a couple more things to finish, den dey're comin' ta be with dere mama.

Within a minute of the kids going upstairs, Betsy overheard raised voices and raced up the steps.

"I get dis room." Peter hollered.

"Nope," Kaylee and Jenny whined. "We got here first, so it's ours."

"Move!" Peter pushed them aside.

"Me and Joseph slept in da room right here in da old house and we're gonna have it now."

"No," Kaylee stamped her foot.

"Stop it, all ya'll. Yer gonna have da same rooms

as before, and dat's final. You girls get dat room, and da boys have dis one. Hailey's is in da corner." Betsy calmly explained without raising her voice.

Lips poked out, and eyes dropped to the floor.

"If ya have da energy ta fight…" Betsy reminded them.

"Ya have da energy ta help." The siblings finished.

"Now, if you're done fightin', dere's things ya'll can do beside startin' World War III in da hallway."

~

Betsy sat down hard on the last tote of leftover linens. *Dere. Now, what am I gonna do with all dis stuff? Hmm. I know. Send it all to da women's shelter. Dey need help too.*

She picked up her phone and dialed their number.

When the director answered, Betsy cleared her throat. "I got too many blankets, sheets, towels, and curtains. My closets are full. Can ya'll use dis stuff?"

"Of course we can. You are so thoughtful, Betsy. The other ladies are starting over just like you. Any donations will help them get back on their feet."

Feels good ta give back ta someone worse off dan me.

As the sun set on the horizon, Betsy peered through her shiny new windows. *"Thank ya, God, way up dere in da sky. Ya gave me a mighty purty house ta live in. I wish Thomas could see all dis. I miss him.* She sighed and sipped her tea.

The next morning, Betsy woke early, showered, and got ready for church. She sat down to eat breakfast at the brand-new table. *"Thank ya, God, way up dere in da sky,"* she prayed, overwhelmed at the community's kindness.

With her meal over, and her dishes in the first dishwasher she ever owned, she happily drove to the church.

"Good mornin,' Preacher man." Betsy gave the minister a firm handshake. She turned to Deborah. "I'm so happy to see ya." Betsy caught her in a bear hug nearly knocking Deborah off her feet. *This was a bad morning to wear heels. I'll show up in sandals next week and shock everyone. Betsy Freeman's rubbing off on me.*

After Betsy took a few steps toward the sanctuary, she spotted Joseph in the Freeman Family Row.

"Wait a minute. How'd he get here?"

"He got released on Friday, but I kept it a secret." Pastor Johnson grinned widely.

"Yay! My baby boy…" Betsy bolted down the aisle like a horse shooting out of the gate at the races.

As she flew by, the ladies did not have to fan their handkerchiefs to keep the odors away. Betsy's wake smelled like roses and talc.

When she reached the front, Joseph stood and grabbed her into a hug, while Betsy laid a slobbery kiss on the cheek.

"Moooom, you're embarrassin' me!" Joseph took a swipe with his hand.

She instantly burst out singing an off-key version of "Rejoice! Rejoice! My son is coming home again."

"Sorry, folks," she apologized then sat down grinning from ear to ear. Miz Pennington did not object this time.

21 Joseph and Betsy Reunited

Betsy stood at the kitchen window waiting for Joseph to come for his first weekend visit.

She held the crumpled letter in her hand. "*Betsy has done an amazing job of keeping her house clean. She showed proof of her seriousness about her second chance. All Betsy's requirements are met. I recommend reunification with her children to be in their best interest. Felicity Wells.*"

Then, she saw a van pull up the driveway and stop beside the house. *Joseph!* She raced to the door and threw it wide open; jumped down the steps two at a time, and hugged Joseph's neck. Then, she greeted all her other children with the same warmth.

It's happenin'. My babies are comin' back home ta me.

The other children climbed back into Mrs. Baker's van. *Their turn's a'comin', and I can't wait.*

When Betsy and Joseph stepped inside the house, the scent of furniture polish and pine hung heavily in the air.

"Oh, Mama, dis place is so nice and clean, and so purty."

Betsy blushed. "I 'spect ta keep it dis way. Why don't ya take yer things ta da bedroom? We'll eat a snack when ya come back downstairs."

"Where's my room?"

"Same place as before. Peter fought like a tiger for dat."

"Good for him. It's just us against all da girls." He chuckled.

When he came back downstairs, she said, "Joseph, you have no idea how hard dis has been for me ta get to dis place. I'd do it all over again. Dat includes sendin' your dad where he cud get help." To emphasize the point, she walked into the kitchen. "Look at dese," Betsy showed him a framed certificate for completing all twelve of the parenting classes. Then, she turned to the dry-erase calendar in the kitchen which had her appointments written neatly. "Dis will help me keep track of stuff. When ya have somethin' goin' on, it goes here."

"Ya hungry?" Betsy already knew the answer before he said anything. *Boys are always hungry.*

"Starved. What's ta eat? " Joseph opened the refrigerator door. "Wow! Lots ta choose from. Not like before." He filled a plate and then stuck it into the microwave. The food popped and made a mess.

"Mama, where's da stuff ta clean dis up?"

Betsy handed him an all-purpose cleaner and a rag. "Thanks for doin' dat. It makes life easier when we clean up after ourselves. Throw da rag in da basket on top of da washer when you're done. Put da cleaner on da supply shelf."

Joseph obeyed. *Life's gonna be different. Mama didn't yell nor curse at me like she used to.*

~

Joseph and his court-appointed probation officer, Mr. Franklin, met for his scheduled session. "Glad to see that you are doing so well. Keep it up."

Joseph smiled. *It feels good to not hear raised voices. Da guards always screamed at us. Mama did too before…*

"The first goal is to stay out of trouble. Do you have a plan yet?"

Joseph shook his head and dropped his eyes toward the floor.

"The file states that you turned sixteen last month. You're old enough to work part-time and begin paying your way in life."

"Who wants ta hire a juvie offender? I tried ta get work before, but everyone laughed at me. What if dey make fun of me again?" Joseph looked away and cracked his knuckles.

"Take that risk. This time is different. You paid the debt to society by serving the sentence in juvie. Lessons were learned, and the track record shows that you do not want to reoffend. It has created character in you. There is such a thing as second chances. Take it and stay out of trouble."

"I gotta do better dan my dad. Don't want my future kids goin' thru what I did."

"I like you already, Joseph. You're going to make something of yourself. I can feel it in my bones."

After a moment, Joseph abruptly stood. "My mom's here."

"Same time next week?"

"I'll be here." Joseph walked to the door, and the officer opened it, and then led him to the waiting area where Betsy sat in the corner fidgeting with her purse strap.

When they got to the car, Joseph piped up. "Mr. Franklin wants me ta work dis summer ta keep me outta trouble."

"Dat's a clever idea. I can't be dere ta watch yer every move when I'm workin'."

They headed to the library. Each of them went to a computer station to look for *Help Wanted* ads. Nothing for unskilled workers.

"What do I do now?" Joseph's forehead wrinkled.

They drifted off into thought for a moment. Then an idea came to Betsy in a flash. "Why don't I talk ta da manager at da bakery?" They hopped into the car and pulled up with a jerk.

Before getting out, Joseph turned to his mother. "Pastor J taught me ta pray when I need somethin'. We can try, can't we?"

"Sure." Betsy started, "God way up dere in da sky, Ya see dis here boy of mine needs a job. Wud Ya have work fer him here? Amen."

"He's gonna answer." Joseph smiled.

When they came back through the doors, both were grinning from ear to ear. "God done it!" Joseph shouted and pumped his fist into the air.

"It's gonna be tough waking up at 3:00 in da mornin,' but I can get used to it. Juvie had a 5:30 roll call."

"Ya have ta go ta bed with da chickens ta hit da deck before da sun breaks over da horizon." Betsy informed him.

~

Felicity signed the paperwork to make his visit become a permanent placement with Betsy because Joseph got a job quickly.

That summer, Joseph did not have an opportunity to get in trouble. Besides working at the bakery full-time, Pastor Johnson's son, Evan, helped him join the youth group at church. As a part of his probation requirements, he had to have adult supervision with him at all events, but he did not care. His troubles were behind him. *No more dope-selling! Not gonna touch da stuff again!*

He grew in his relationship with God and everyone around him, and he was happy.

22 Hailey the Protector

After Joseph settled into his routine, then it was Hailey's turn to come home. On Friday, Mrs. Baker dropped her off. *Mama! How much I've missed you.* Hailey raced up the porch steps and ran headlong into her mother's open arms.

"It's good to be home." Hailey sighed.

That night, she stretched out on her brand-new bed. *AHH! No springs pokin' through da mattress ta scratch me like my old bed did. No buckets sittin' here an' dere collectin' rainwater, goin' drip, drip, drip all night long.*

She picked up her cell phone and dialed Vanessa Johnson's number. "Hey, it's me. I'm home finally." After talking for an hour, she hung up and smiled.

'Tis good ta have a friend. She closed her eyes and drifted off to sleep.

Since her mama and Joseph worked an early shift, she knew that Grandma Caroline would be there when she woke up.

The next morning, Hailey automatically made her

bed then gathered the laundry, and carried it downstairs. She went into the bathrooms and grabbed the towels, then got her mom's dirty clothes. By that time, Grandma Caroline had descended the steps. The washer swished away with the first load. "Laundry was my chore on Saturdays at Mrs. Baker's house, so I'm used to it."

After they talked and laughed for a long while, Grandma Caroline looked at the clock. "Oops. Where did the time go? We need to fix a brunch for your mom and Joseph."

Hailey stood and walked into the kitchen. "What should we make?" They both like omelets, but I don't know how ta make dem."

"Check the fridge to see what you have."

Hailey pulled several items out and placed them on the counter. "My mama likes peppers, onions, cheese, and bacon." She lifted the frying pan down from off its hook.

"Okay, here is what you do." Grandma Caroline gave her step-by-step directions, and the omelets turned out perfectly.

"Now, you need to add a carbohydrate such as bread."

"Texas toast?" Hailey pulled a pack out and put it in the microwave to thaw, then placed them on a baking sheet to brown in the oven.

By the time Hailey finished, the back door unlocked, and Betsy and Joseph entered.

"Mmm. Somethin' smells good." Betsy walked into the dining room where Hailey finished setting the table.

When they sat down, she bowed her head and

repeated the prayer which Mrs. Baker taught her.

"Thank ya for doin' dat. We need to say dat at all da meals." Betsy patted her daughter's hand. "Ya learned so much dere."

"Mrs. Baker taught me how ta do lotsa bakin' and cookin', but she always fixed breakfast."

"Dis omelet is good. Who taught ya ta do dis?" Joseph swallowed his first bite.

Hailey beamed. "Grandma Caroline."

After her mother and Joseph headed upstairs to nap, and her grandma left, Hailey changed the laundry loads and cleaned up the kitchen. Then, she plopped down on the pillowy-soft couch and drifted off into a dream world.

Hailey startled awake to a loud persistent knock on the back door. She peered through the peephole. Bobby, their troublesome neighbor stood on the other side. "Whaddya want?" She yelled.

"Need ta see Joseph."

"He's not comin' out now or ever, so ya stay away from my brother, ya snot-nosed troublemaker!"

Bobby kept knocking.

"I'll call da police if'n ya keep it up," Hailey warned.

He ignored her, and she kept her word. The sheriff arrived in record time and hauled Bobby away.

"Good job, Hailey," Joseph whispered behind her. You're da Family Protector."

She beamed.

"Bobby got what he deserved. He knows he can't be around here."

If'n he comes again, I'll have Mama put a No Contact order on him." Joseph declared.

"Thanks. Bobby's nothin' but trouble. I hate ridin' home on da school bus with him." Hailey's face reddened. "I think he has a crush on me."

"Don't ya dare think about datin' dat bug-eyed little creep, or I'll have to pound da both of ya!"

"No need to worry. I can't stand his guts."

"Good. Keep it dat way. No two-bit druggie is welcome here."

"Thanks."

Changing the subject, Joseph asked, "What are we havin' for lunch? I'm starved again."

"Guys! Always thinkin' of food." She playfully shoved him, turned, and walked toward the kitchen.

~

After Betsy got up from her nap, she was surprised to see that Hailey and Joseph had done the Saturday chores. She glanced out at the newly mown lawn. *Joseph musta done dat while Hailey did the household chores. Not a speck of dust anywhere. And dere's a fresh blueberry pie just waitin' fer us ta attack it. I'm impressed!*

"Great job, both of ya. Let's go ta Dairy Shoppe for a treat. "

"Oh, yeah!" they responded.

~

Since it was still summertime, Hailey got into a routine. Wake up, shower, do chores, then fix Joseph's and her mom's breakfast. On two afternoons a week, she spent time with Vanessa Johnson, the pastor's daughter. They often helped Mrs. Hudson at the soup kitchen. On Fridays, Grandma Caroline took her to the grocery store with a list from Betsy.

"Here's da budget for food dis week. Make it

stretch," her mom instructed her before they left to do the grocery buying.

Grandma took the time to teach Hailey how to comparison shop, check unit prices, and watch for sale items. "Buying food is always about being savvy and wise," she said. "You're smart as a whip."

Hailey shrugged. "It's a lot like detective work. Ya look for da clues to da best prices. I should buy a magnifyin' glass and hat like Sherlock Holmes." They laughed.

When they got back home, Hailey unloaded the groceries, and put everything in its place, then plopped down on the couch.

No wonder Mama's tired when she gets done with shoppin'.

23 Peter Learns the Hard Way.

Peter's arrival home was like a hand grenade thrown into a calm lake. Things that had lain peacefully under the surface exploded into the air. The harmony and quiet of the home slipped away with each slamming door, and scream. He had tossed aside everything he learned at Mrs. Baker's house, and was intent on causing as much trouble as he could.

"Why should I have ta clean dat up when it's yer job? Girls were born ta take care of da guys." Peter screamed at Hailey.

"Who told ya dat nonsense? It ain't my mess. It's yers. Mama's rules are, if'n ya make messes, ya gotta clean dem up." Hailey huffed.

"I don't gotta listen to ya, so dere." Peter stuck out his tongue and blew raspberries at her.

Hearing the ruckus in the living room, Betsy silently slipped in. "Hey, what's goin' on? And why is yer tongue stickin' outta yer head? Ya tryin' ta catch flies with dat? Boy, stick it back in, or so help me, I'll put it on fire with a dose of red pepper."

Peter complied, taken aback at his mama's innovative approach to problems without cursing and threatening.

"Now, clean up dat mess, den ya earned da task of pulling weeds in da flower beds. Go." Betsy pointed at the exit. "It better be done right, or ya get ta do it over again." Peter slammed the screen door.

"Get back here, son. Ya close it right." She stared him down.

He sulked but obeyed.

After weeks of his acting out, Joseph confronted Peter. "What's up, man? Why are ya doin' all dis ta us? Don'tcha wanna be here?"

Peter hung his head. "I'm tired of Hailey bossin' me around."

"Why wud ya say dat? She looks out for ya just like before, so what's changed?"

"She gets to go out, and I'm stuck here with no friends my age."

"Ya poor baby. She's older dan ya and has earned da right ta a little break now and den. Hailey works hard to keep the laundry clean, and cooks when Mama is busy. On her off days, she's serving da community at da soup kitchen. That's why we have Styrofoam meals twice a week." Joseph stuck up for his sister. "Besides, Ya could talk to me." Joseph encouraged.

"Bout what? Yer never around, always sleepin', workin', or hangin' out with yer friends. Anyway, we're always doin' chores. I'm not a baby anymore." Peter stomped his foot and scowled.

"So, stop actin' like one. Unless ya quit dese shenanigans, ya may end up in juvie as I did."

"Den, maybe I should go dere." Peter turned red

and bit his tongue.

"Whoa! Hold on a sec. What did ya just say?"

"Bobby and me have been sellin' hot stuff online." Peter hesitantly admitted.

"Whaddya mean?"

"We drive around, and watch houses dat nobody's home, den swoop in and snatch what we can get our hands on, like money, packages, TVs, and stuff like dat. It's kinda fun ta keep da old copperheads guessin' where we'll strike next."

"So, dat's where ya been sneakin' off to after dark."

"Yep." Peter proudly proclaimed. "Nobody knows, so ya better keep it quiet."

"How much money have ya made doin' dis?" Joseph prodded.

"Bout a thousand bucks."

"Really? And ya learned nothin' by my bein' in da slammer?" Joseph's voice raised for a moment, then he took a deep cleansing breath.

"Don't tell Mama or Hailey." Peter begged.

"Dat's not gonna happen, Peter. I gotta tell cuz I'm on probation. Yer dancin' with danger, and ya know it. What if'n someone has a gun waitin' ta blow yer head off?"

"Didn't think of dat. So, ya gonna turn me in?"

"We're gonna talk to Mama, den go from dere."

Peter knew the jig was up. His shoulders slumped as he followed Joseph to the living room.

"Mom, Peter's gotta say somethin'."

"Go ahead. Tell me," Betsy encouraged.

When he confessed, she was madder that a cat thrown into a pool. "Why would ya do dis? Haven't we been in enough trouble?" Betsy squalled loud enough to echo for a country mile.

Peter shivered. *When she gets dis mad, terrible things happen.*

Betsy paused and wiped her tears. "Okay. Sit down on da couch, and don't ya dare move an inch." She dialed her phone, then they waited.

When the police and Felicity Wells arrived, Betsy blurted. "Peter will tell ya what he and dat nasty neighbor Bobby's been doin'. Stand up an' tell da truth."

Peter shakily stood to his feet. "Bobby and me been swipin' and sellin' stuff on eBay."

"Why?" Sergeant Turner looked him squarely in the eyes.

Peter shrugged.

The police officer turned to the caseworker. "Miss Wells, what is your policy about this?"

"He must go into custody until the judge sees him."

"Very well," Sergeant Turner opened the door. "Come with me, young man." He motioned to Peter. "Let's go."

Dumb ole' Joseph got me in trouble. He's gonna pay for dis.

When the police car went down the driveway, Betsy sobbed. "Where'd I go so wrong? I done my best ta get ya kids back, now he's done gone and did dis stupid thing."

Felicity encouraged her. "You have done everything right. Peter is the one who caused trouble, not you."

Joseph slipped his arm around his mama's

shoulders. "Peter needs to learn ta stay outta trouble. He can choose ta behave or not. It's up ta him. Let's pray for him right now. Jesus, Peter messed up just like I did. He followed me an' I don't like dat. He knows how to do better. He isn't thinkin' straight. He's missin' his dad just like I am. We all miss him, but we got no excuses to do wrong. Show him a better way to deal with stuff. Amen."

"Thank ya, Joseph. Dat was so nice." Betsy leaned her head on his shoulder.

I've been through fire and brimstone to get da kids back. Didn't deserve dis. I'll plow through dis like every other thing dat's comes my way. Nobody shakes me, not even my kids.

~

Hailey spoke up after remaining silent throughout the whole ordeal. "Maybe we cud get Peter ta do somethin' dat wud keep him busy."

"Like what?"

Hailey had their attention now. "Peter loves animals. I've watched him splint the leg of one of the barn cats. And it stopped limpin' in a few weeks. He's a different kid when he does dat stuff."

"How'd I miss dat." Betsy interrupted her.

"I was around him more when you were workin' at the diner. He's been doin' dis stuff since he was six or seven years old."

"Dat's a great idea, Hailey. When did ya get so smart?"

She grinned but didn't respond.

~

With his hands behind his back and flanked by police officers, Peter trembled as they led him to the juvenile booking center.

Is dis what it's like for Dad? Not sure I like it so much.

He fidgeted and looked around the precinct.

"What's your name, kid?"

Crickets!

"Excuse me." Sergeant Turner pulled him to his feet and stared directly into his face. "Cooperate, or I'll inform Judge Brown about how you're acting."

Better play along, or I'll be here when Dad gets out. I can't do dat though I miss him like crazy.

He cleared his throat. "Peter Freeman."

"Good. Now we're getting somewhere. And you're eleven, right?"

"Yep." Peter gulped.

The sergeant frisked him. "What do we have here?" He pulled a large wad of cash out of Peter's jeans pocket. "That's a lot of do-re-me for a kid. Where'd you get all this?"

I better tell da truth. "I earned it."

"How? Not by selling newspapers, I gather."

"Nah, I help someone, and dey pay me."

"Go on. The more you cooperate, the better it will be in the morning."

"I help a neighbor with his business."

"What kind of business?"

Peter began to sweat profusely. "Um, Bobby'll kill me if I tell ya what he does."

"We'll protect you if you need us to, but you must tell the truth."

Peter could no longer hold back and blurted out the whole story of the thefts.

"Okay. That's enough for now. Since this is your

first offense, the judge might be understanding.”

But Mama won't be!

Subdued and scared out of his mind, the officers led Peter to the holding cell where he waited for daylight to come.

The next morning, Peter stood in front of Judge Brown to face the music for what he'd done, but he wasn't alone. Behind him sat his family, Grandma Caroline, and Felicity Wells. It calmed his nerves when he looked up at the scowling official.

“Young man,” Judge Brown firmly spoke, “You're headed down a slippery slope to prison. Is that where you want to be for the rest of your life? Think hard!”

“No, judge.” Peter looked him in the eyes.

“Then stop getting into trouble. You have three counts against you…B&E, handling, and selling stolen goods. You are a juvenile delinquent. This does not bode well.” Judge Brown stared at him.

“Stay away from your neighbor. He's bad news.

“I have a deal for you since we have confiscated the money that was in your possession. Go with Sergeant Turner and point out every house that you entered. You will knock on the doors and apologize. Secondly, you will lead the police to the place where you stored the stolen items. You tell him which pawn shop you visited, and where you listed the things online. And last, you will be on probation for six months with work detail through the Junior Youth Services Program at the Duncan Farm for the rest of the summer. They'll supply room and board for you in exchange for work. If you don't work, you don't eat. It is as simple as that. Do we have a deal?”

“Yes, sir.” Peter wiped his eyes on his sleeve.

"There will be a five-minute recess for the next case," declared Judge Brown, who had been fair and merciful.

Peter ran to his mama. "I'm sorry." He wept.

"It's okay, son. You had to learn da hard way like yer daddy did."

"No more actin' up, ya hear?" Betsy kissed his cheek.

"I'll behave."

"Great. Sergeant Turner is waiting."

Peter turned and went with him out of the courthouse.

Suddenly, he was too busy to think about getting into trouble. Besides working on Duncan Farm, he enrolled in 4-H, and had to meet with his probation officer every week.

Peter wrote letters home filled with adventures of farm life. *"I got to see a calf born dis mornin'. Dere are lots of chores here, and we gotta get up at 3:30 in da morning cuz dere's milkin' and hayin' and all kinds of stuff. It's fun, but I get so tired."*

PS. I'm sorry. Peter

Betsy sniffled and wiped her eyes after reading his letter. *God way up in da sky is takin' care of him. Peter's learnin' da hard way, but he's in a place where he can learn.*

24 All Together Again

By the middle of September, Kaylee and Jenny went home with their mother on a trial basis. When Mrs. Baker's van pulled up the driveway for the last time, Betsy raced down the steps.

My babies... Dey're finally back under my roof, and nobody is ever gonna take dem away again. Now, please, God way up dere in da sky, help me ta do it right. It's gonna be harder now dat da girls are back with me.

"Mama, can ya help me with my homework?" Jenny called from the dining room table.

Betsy glanced down at the math sheets. "Oooh boy, here we go! "Let's see what we can do." She grabbed some scrap paper, sat down beside her, and wrote the problem on her paper.

"Ya try ta work it same time as me," Betsy encouraged. *If only my mama'd done dat with me. I ain't gonna be like her.* She put her arm around the back of Jenny's chair. *Poor girl struggles like I did.* Betsy explained each step as they worked the problems, and their answers matched the key in the back of the math book.

When they were finally through, the sun had gone down, and everyone was hungry. Betsy went to the refrigerator. "Chili okay for supper?"

"Yeah."

While Betsy and Hailey cooked the meal, Peter went out to the barn to make sure to secure Buttercup, his 4-H calf, for the night.

When he came back inside, he declared, "Looks like a storm's brewin'. Da wind has picked up, and da moon has a close ring around it."

"Supper's ready now, so we'll make sure we're prepared for it. Come, sit down at the table."

After the meal, Betsy said, "Ya'll better get da homework done before da lights go off.

"Jenny, you have clean-up duty and dishes while I get Kaylee ready for bed."

Jenny nodded and obeyed her mother.

Betsy took Kaylee upstairs and ran the water for her bath, then laid out her pajamas and a pull-up for her. *I'm so glad Mrs. Baker told me what to do to help with the bed-wetting issue. The doctor said she's doin' it cuz everythin' is topsy turvy in our world. She'll grow out of it in a few years. I hope so anyhow. If not, dere may be somethin' wrong, and I can't think bout dat right now.*

Betsy and Kaylee went downstairs, and while Kaylee went into the living room, she walked to the window. *Peter was right. Da storm was a'comin'. The sky's all black and spooky.*

The banging, crashing thunder roared furiously, sizzling, chain lightning illuminated the night sky.

Heavy rain fell from the heavens in sheets. The lights flickered and went out. Betsy lit the emergency candle on the coffee table.

She could see the children curled up on chairs and couch alike, burrowed under blankets and wraps.

Nobody spoke. The crack of thunder drowned out any sounds they could make.

"Dis one's a doozy," Betsy interrupted the silence.

Kaylee clung to her shaking nervously. "Are we gonna be okay, Mama?"

"Yeah, Honey. God way up dere in da sky is takin' lovin' care of us. We're safe and dry. Nothin' bad's gonna happen." Betsy spoke with confidence that she didn't have.

Kaylee didn't respond because she felt safe and warm curled up in her Mama's arms.

In an hour, the rain slowed to a drizzle, and the electricity came back on. It was late when Betsy sent them all to bed. "Good night ya'll. Sleep well."

Early in the morning, when she got ready for work, the fog lay heavily all around. She woke Joseph up. "Come on. We need ta leave A.S.A.P. Da fog's as thick as pea soup."

"Be dere in a few." He yawned and threw his covers back.

"I got a breakfast wrap ready for ya ta eat in da car."

Betsy's windshield wipers swished so fast that they nearly flew off the window.

She slid her seat as close as she could to the steering wheel. Suddenly, she hit a patch of wet leaves on the roadway. Betsy slammed on the brakes and slid off the side of the road. Her heart was in her throat. "Ya okay, Joseph?"

"Yeah. What about ya?"

"I'm alright."

Betsy put the car in reverse and spun her wheels. With a firm grip on the gravel, she gradually made her way back onto the highway.

"Better slow down a bit," Betsy said as she concentrated on the road in front of her. She blew out a huge breath when they pulled into the bakery's employee parking lot.

"Today was a bit scary," Joseph piped up.

"God way up in da sky kept us safe when it could've been much worse."

25 God, Can I Get a Do-Over?

Nighttime was the worst for Betsy because she hated sleeping by herself. Sometimes, Kaylee would come downstairs and cuddle up to her. It was comforting to have her little body next to hers. The only drawback was that Kaylee always kicked like a mule at night and hogged all the covers. *Thomas never did that. He may have been a drunk, but at least he was there. Now, as a single parent to five kids, it's like going across a burning swing bridge with a monkey on my back.*

When they were all in school, Betsy would have a good, old-fashioned sob-fest. After her tears dried on her cheeks, she felt Jesus's whisper to her heart. *"Betsy, you aren't alone. I'm here."*

She would dry her eyes and look up. *"God way up dere in da sky, bein' a single mom ain't easy."*

"I know. I understand. If you'll let Me, I'll put your load on My shoulders."

"Please, I need Ya ta do dat. Sometimes, life gets ta be too much. I have ta get up so early in da mornin'

ta go ta work, den come home to da daily grind. If da world spun any faster, I'd fall off."

Jesus continued. *"Life is a marathon, not a sprint. Take time to enjoy the special moments with your children, the talks with Caroline, and the porch chats with Miz Pennington. Do not be too hard on yourself. You are not superwoman."*

She chuckled. *"No, I'm just plain ole Betsy doin' all I can."*

"That's all I expect."

Betsy's heart felt comforted, and her courage returned. *"I can do dis."*

"Of course, you can," Jesus whispered.

Then Betsy's thoughts turned to Thomas, and her mind took her through an unhappy journey of pain and heartache. She remembered times when he would grab her roughly and pull her onto the ragged couch. Then, he'd laugh drunkenly as she struggled against his sloppy unwanted kisses. His breath was strong enough to make an iron stomach do flip-flops. He'd be apologetic, but it only lasted a day or two, then he was back to his drinking and beating.

Betsy had to be careful what she wore in those days because cheap make-up could not cover black and blue very well. Even in the summer, she never wore cotton because the gentle breezes might uncover her secret.

Betsy suffered taunts and cruel stares wherever she went. She never felt feminine or pretty, but like an object instead of a person. And certainly not as a princess. She opened her top dresser drawer, and then pulled out her favorite nightie and smiled. She loved how the fabric felt in her fingers. Betsy recalled the magical way that Thomas grinned at her with that special gleam in his eyes.

How could one man and one set of hands deliver pleasure and pain at the same time?

Betsy's eyes welled up with tears as she folded the nightie and put it away. *"God way up dere in da sky, can I get a do-over with Thomas?... Da one with kind hands and lovin' touches, not da ogre who punches holes in da wall and hurts my kids. Is dat too much ta ask?"* Betsy slid to the side of her bed, rocking back and forth, slowly letting her anger and pain flow out of her.

Her spirit quieted, and she breathed in deeply. She was about ready to get up when she felt the warmth of a hug. Betsy looked around. No one else was in the room.

"God way up dere in da sky, was dat You?"

"Yes."

Betsy stopped rocking.

"Do you remember in Sunday School when Miz Pennington talked about My love for you?"

"Hm-hmm."

"The picture of the Great Shepherd with a little lamb in His arms hung in your Sunday School room."

"Yeah, I always liked dat picture."

"Thomas is the tiny sheep I am carrying in my arms. He had open wounds in his heart when I found him. I took him into My fold. Go ask Miz Pennington about the story of the Good Shepherd."

After that conversation, Betsy drove across town to her former Sunday School teacher's house. Her memories flooded back as she used to sneak away from her abusive mother to listen to the stories from the Bible on Miz Pennington's porch swing.

Many times, Miz Pennington would dry her tears and bandage her wounds, but she could never heal the emotional injuries deep within her heart.

She opened her car door and started up the walk.

"Well, if it ain't Betsy Fallon." The old woman stood to her feet and hobbled across the porch. "Come on up here and sit a spell."

Betsy smiled. *Nobody ever calls me by my birth name anymore.*

"What's on your mind?" Alma Pennington never beat around the bush.

"God way up dere in da sky told me ta ask ya bout da Good Shepherd and what it means."

"Let's get some tea, then we can talk." Miz Pennington went inside and brought out a tray with two steaming cups and a plate of Betsy's favorite Snickerdoodle cookies. She opened her Bible and began the story as they enjoyed the fall afternoon.

"In the New Testament, Jesus told the Scribes and Pharisees a story. There was a man who had one hundred sheep and as he was doing his nightly count, he got to ninety-nine. 'Hmm, one of the lambs is missing. Better find it before the wolves do.' So, he left his other sheep safely in the hands of the Under-Shepherds and went off looking for it. 'Wooly, where are you?'"

"His name wasn't Wooly, was it?" Betsy interrupted.

"I had to give him a name. Shall I continue?"

"Please." Betsy heard the story before, but nobody except Miz Pennington could tell it right.

"After hours of searching, the Good Shepherd found Wooly. 'Come here, you naughty one. Let's go home.' The Shepherd picked up Wooly and held him close to His heart. He walked back over the dangerous path in the moonlight, until Wooly was safe with his mother."

Betsy listened with rapt attention, forgetting the plate of cookies. "Ya mean dat da Good Shepherd went lookin' for me an' Thomas cuz we were not in His flock?"

"That's right."

"He didn't want ole split hoof to have you. Now you both belong to Him."

"I get it." Betsy brightened, paused, then changed the subject.

"Why are ya so nice ta me and my family?"

"Well, my husband was a lot like yours, so I understand what you're going through."

"Did yer husband beat ya and yer kids?"

"Yes. He was an unfaithful, violent scoundrel. The children suffered a lot because of his behavior, but we felt relief instead of sadness when he died in an accident at work."

"Do yer kids ever come around?"

"Sometimes."

Betsy took a sip of her tea.

"It's been a while." Miz Pennington's gaze lifted far away.

They sat in silence for several minutes, deep in their thoughts, until Betsy broke the stillness.

"Do ya think Thomas'll want ta come home after his year is up? I still love him, but he ain't gonna hit da kids an' me anymore. My house, my rules."

"Have you written to him?" Miz Pennington sipped her tea.

"Nah. No contact means just dat. I can't talk ta him." Betsy's words bubbled and gurgled out of her mouth like she had swallowed shampoo. Tears flowed down her cheeks as she babbled on. "What if he never comes back? I'll be a single mom forever." The sobbing intensified in pitch until she was squalling like an alley cat at night.

"No, you won't. This year will pass quickly, so don't ever second-guess your decisions. I wish I would have had your courage. Things would have been better for ya."

"What do ya mean?"

"My husband had a one-night stand with your mother after the county square dance. We didn't think anything about it until she showed us the results."

"How come ya ain't told me til now?" Betsy stood up quickly and backed toward the steps.

Miz Pennington shrugged. "It mortified me. How could he do that? Yet, in the whole mix was a baby girl that looked exactly like her daddy. Your mother hated that and took it out on you."

Betsy sat back down.

Miz Pennington continued. "Your mama orchestrated everything to get someone to support her, so she didn't have to work. Since there was no child support order set up by the courts, she'd show up and demand cash on a whim. If Hans would hesitate, she'd threaten to go to the police and tell them that it was rape, which was a lie. She seduced Hans when he was drunk."

"She didn't spend money on me, so where'd da cash go?"

"When you were sleeping, she'd hit the bars all

night."

"I don't want ta talk about her anymore. She was always throwin' up, and her head hurt her bad. Serves her right. I'd had ta take care of her like she were a tiny tot."

Betsy scowled.

Miz Pennington sucked in a huge breath. "No use crying over spilled milk. They are both gone now, and the past is where it is supposed to be. Besides, you have more integrity in your little finger than both Hans and Bertha put together."

Betsy sat stunned and silent.

"Well, the good news is that I'm technically your stepmom." Miz Pennington tried to bring a positive spin on the shocking information.

Betsy's eyes widened with wonder. "And dat means my kids have two grandmas."

"Yes." Now tears flowed down both their cheeks. "I wanted to tell ya a long time ago, but I couldn't. You were already going through enough, so I did the best I could."

"What's dat?"

"Pray and love you unconditionally. I knew that one day, God would let me explain the situation to you."

Betsy smiled. "I'm glad ya prayed. It helped so much. Prayer could help Thomas too."

"He's on my special list."

"Talkin' of Thomas, is dere any way ta find out about him?" Betsy leaned in closer to get any scrap of information.

"He is all right. Pastor Johnson told the Prayer Warriors that he finished the Sober Living Program at

Riftwood and is now at Brock's Home. He wants to reunite with his family."

"Does he now?" Betsy blushed. "Thanks for talkin'."

"It's okay. Ya can chew the fat with me anytime. Ya know where my front porch is."

They laughed. "I need ta find it more often, huh step-mom?" Betsy stood. "Kids will be home from school soon, so I need to go."

"Don't be a stranger, ya hear?" Miz Pennington stood and grabbed her cane.

Betsy drove home, singing at the top of her lungs. *Wait til I tell da kids bout dis! Dey're not gonna believe it. Two grandmas. Wowzers!*

26 Dear Thomas

That night after the kids were in bed, Betsy sat at the dining room table and sipped tea. The brand-new notebook lay open in front of her. The page had two words written at the top. *Dear Thomas.*

She stared at the lined sheet in front of her and pulled it closer. Her heart pounded loudly in her ears. *I gotta try dis. Hope I don't get in trouble.*

Dear Thomas, Yer on my mind day and night. Ya are a long way away from me and da kids, and we miss ya so much. Dere actin' up some cuz ya ain't here. Peter specially keeps gettin' in trouble. He needs a daddy to help rein him in. He had to go to Duncan Farm for weeks and weeks cuz he was stealin' and lyin'. I was madder dan an old wet hen when he told me what he and Bobby was doin'.

Joseph's back home with me, in fact all da kids are. Everybody's home 'cept for ya. Many nights I lay there with my eyeballs wide open wonderin' how ya been. It hurts all of us ta be apart from ya. We're countin' down da days. Seems like forever until the year's up. I didn't wanna be mean to ya like my Mama was to me, but dere wasn't any way else to wake ya up, so ya cud see da bad path ya were walkin' down.

This old girl had to go through some stuff too. I looked in da mirror one day and saw my Mama lookin' back at me. Her ugly ole self showed in how I talked to ya and da kids. Dat was da time God, way up dere in da sky told me dat I cud make changes. No way cud I do it by myself. He had to do it for me.

I asked Him into my heart, and He did da changin'. If'n He can forgive me, den I gotta forgive ya for all da stuff ya have done to me and da kids. No more blamin' ya for everythin'. I had a part too. Da drinkin' got us all in trouble. We've been thru a lot, but deep inside I love ya and forgive ya for everythin'. Nothin's gonna take dat away.

Silent tears fell and splashed onto the paper leaving big wet blotches. Before the ink was dry on one side, she flipped it over and wrote like her pen was on fire. Pages of dampened paper appeared on the stack of her written thoughts. Finally, after her heart was at peace, she signed the letter. *I love ya ta da moon and back. I miss ya so much. Betsy.*

Exhausted, she took the notebook and stuffed the letter inside, then shoved it into her top drawer where the children couldn't find it.

Betsy put on her favorite nightie, grabbed Thomas's pillows, and cuddled up close hoping to have pleasant dreams, not the terrorizing nightmares she had had since Thomas went away.

She said her nighttime prayers. "God way up dere in da sky, can ya be with Thomas? We need him here so bad. Help him ta be strong enough ta not drink again."

As soon as she fell asleep, something woke her. *What's dat?* Her heart beat like a racehorse rounding the last turn. She threw her robe on and grabbed her gun from the hidden locked box. *Nobody's gonna mess with me or my kids. So, help me, I'll make dem look like a junk yard dog with a few missin' pieces gone.*

She opened the bedroom door swiftly to catch the intruder by surprise. She looked around. Adrenaline raced through her body. She was on high alert. The gun cocked in her right hand. Slowly, she slipped down the hall with her heartbeat pounding in her ears. *Be brave, Betsy.*

She inched forward toward the open door and waved the gun around like she was a police officer. "Who's dere?" She yelled. "Ya better come out with da hands up or yer guts are gonna hang from dat yonder tree."

"It's just me, Mom." Peter stepped out of the shadows. "Thought I heard somethin' in da barn."

She nodded and tightened her grip on the gun. "I got da safety on, but I find anybody lurkin', I'll blow dem ta da middle of next week."

"Shh." Peter put his finger to his lips. "Hear dat?" *Rustle! Scratch! Bump!*

Betsy nodded as they snuck to the barn. "The sound's comin' from da feed room." She whispered.

Sliding quietly inside they shone the lights around until they rested on two beady little eyes. "Stupid raccoon!" Peter declared disgustedly.

"Want me ta blast him?"

"Nah. Let's scare him away."

Betsy flipped on the overhead lights, and the coon

scampered into the shadows as fast as his tiny legs would carry him. *Too bad. Dat would've made fine eatin' with a mess of collard greens and a hunk of cornbread.*

"Bummer. He got in da corn again. What am I gonna do?"

"Tomorrow, we'll buy a metal trash bin, so he can't paw his way through." Betsy put her arm around her son. "Why don't you put dat barrel on top of it for tonight?"

When they turned it over, bottles of beer and wine tumbled onto the floor. "Oh, we found one of your dad's hidin' places." Betsy opened each bottle and poured the brew on the ground. "Dis stuff is da curse of da family. Never drink it, Peter."

"I can't stand da smell of it." He wrinkled his nose. "It reminds me of Dad though. I miss him."

"I know. So, do I. Why don't ya write a letter ta him? When yer all bottled up like a shook-up Coke, writin' a letter helps."

"Maybe." Peter soothed his calf, Buttercup, to calm her, then latched the barn door, and they walked into the house together.

"Yer so good with animals, Peter." Betsy closed and locked the door.

~

The next day after work, Betsy drove to the courthouse. "I wanna talk ta Judge Paxton," she told the receptionist.

"Have a seat while I call his office." The girl picked up the phone.

After waiting for an hour, the young woman motioned her to the desk. "The judge will see you now.

Go to the blue elevator and take it up to the third floor."

Betsy scurried off. When she knocked on Judge Paxton's door, she heard his booming voice answering.

"What can I do for you, Mrs. Freeman?" He greeted her warmly. "The kids aren't giving you any trouble, are they?"

"Nah, I have somethin' ta ask ya."

"Go ahead."

"Would it be okay to write letters to Thomas?" Betsy leaned forward in her chair.

"Hmm, you still have quite a while on the No Contact order. Typically, victims do not want that to change. Why do you ask?"

"I miss him so much. Thought it would make us feel better by writin' to each other."

Judge Paxton paused for a few minutes while he looked at his notes about the Freeman cases. "Okay, I can amend the order to only allow letters. No phone calls or any other form of communication. In the meantime, I will send the amendments to your caseworkers."

Betsy stood to her feet. "Thank ya." She was on cloud nine as she rushed outside and let out a whoop on the courthouse steps. But her sunshine became storm clouds when she found a yellow ticket on the windshield of her car.

What's dis? A ticket for an expired meter? Can I ever catch a break? She yanked it off and looked at the time stamp on the ticket then at her watch. *Dey wrote dis five minutes ago. How dare dey! Forty dollars. Dat's highway robbery!*

She put a quarter in the meter and charged like an enraged bull with the yellow ticket flapping in her hand.

Nostrils widened. If one looked close enough, he could see steam coming from her ears as she marched back into the courthouse. She halted, stomping her feet in anger as she read the directory then punched the button on the elevator to the second floor.

"Can I help you?" A little woman with a knot of grey hair on top of her head peeked over the divider at her.

"Yeah. I got a stupid ticket for five minutes over da meter limit!" Betsy bellowed.

"Ma'am, take a deep breath, and I'll help you."

Betsy swallowed the rest of her words.

"You can pay here and be done, or if you want to contest it; you can talk to the traffic court office." She snapped her gum.

Betsy pulled out her wallet and plunked the money on the counter. "I need a receipt." She raced back to her car with two minutes to spare. *Phew! Dat was close.* Betsy burned rubber halfway down the street.

When she got home, she pulled out the letter she had written last night. Betsy read it over before she folded it, slipped it into an envelope, and added the address that Judge Paxton gave her. On the back, she held the letter to her lips and kissed it then wrote *S.W.A.K.* Thomas would know what that meant. With a huge sigh, Betsy stamped it, walked down the driveway to the mailbox, and put the letter inside. After raising the red flag, she strode back up to the house.

I wonder what Thomas will say when he gets dis. Will he write back?

27 Thomas Writes a Letter.

Thomas kept busy. His days filled themselves with work, meetings, classes, and recreation. He attended chapel services on Sundays, then he rested. On Monday morning, he awoke to attack a fresh new week with vigor.

Autumn came with its breath-taking colors. The trees in the greenhouse lost their leaves while chrysanthemums, marigolds, and other fall flowers filled the place with beauty. Thomas happily dealt with the customers. He loved his job, and he worked out a business plan to create a greenhouse on his farm. Brock's Home promised to help him set it up and get the business off the ground. It would mean a lot of demanding work, but he knew that he could do it.

As the holidays approached, melancholy overcame Thomas. He wanted to be at home but still had two months yet. When Mr. Gomez visited him, he mentioned the fact that he desired to be with his family for Christmas Day.

"Let me see what we can do." Mr. Gomez stood to

go. "Have a good week."

~

Thomas checked his mailbox every day hoping that Betsy would break her silence. As usual, nothing ever entered in his box except junk mail. One day, he opened it and found a perfumed letter from her. He danced around the mailroom. "I got a letter." He grinned from ear to ear. He raced upstairs to read the words of the one whom he had abused, yet somehow, she still loved him and wanted what was best for him. *My Betsy...*

One evening, Thomas took a pen and paper then began to write in his best penmanship. His thoughts came from the wellspring deep within his soul. He wrote with vigor and intensity. When he was through, he wept like a baby, but his heart felt at peace.

Dear Betsy, I was so happy ta get yer letter. I'm sorry for hittin' ya and hurtin' ya da way I did. T'wasn't right of me. Shoulda never hurt my kids neither. Is Hailey doin' any better? She weren't happy with me at da sentencin' hearin'. It was my fault dat she has pain. How can I make it up ta ya'll? Gotta say ya made me so mad for sendin' me away, but it were da best thing for me. It made me think. Ya know dat I got dried out. Dem DT shakes and longin' for a drink went away after a while. Had ta go ta Doc Whitney every day and take my pills. If'n I hid dem, dey always find dem and get me in trouble. After a while, I ran outta hidin' places. At first, I didn't wanna get better, but with Paster J comin' and talkin' ta me, I found out dat my grudge against my granny and grandpappy hurt me, not dem. Dey treated me like dirt. The stubborn old coots were just plain mean. When I let go of dat mess, I cud sleep like a baby. Paster J. helped me find Jesus, so I cud forgive dem.

I'm 145 days sober cuz God cleaned me up. At Brock's Home, I learnt ta read after I got a pair of specks. I look edjurcated. And I'm gettin' new chompers. Yer gonna have ta watch out. I'm a brand-new man. Passed my GED, so I can get a job. Dey asked me what I like ta do. Said I wanna play in da dirt. Ha! Ha! Next thing I know, I'm up past my ears in fertilizer in da greenhouse. And I love it. Soon, I'll send money home for ya and da kids. Gotta do right. Dey said if'n I do well here, I might get a day away for Christmas if'n da judge says so.

I hope ta start my business when I come back. I can't wait till my time is up.

Love, Thomas. XOXO PS. Do ya still got dat nightie?

~

Thomas wrote to Betsy and the children every week.

Dear Betsy and family: I miss ya'll so much. Time here at Brock's Home has helped me to be better dan I was. Da counselor said we can turn our life into somethin' good. With da greenhouse I work in, I'm learnin' dat Grandpappy Freeman was wrong. I am good at somethin'. Life is what I make it ta be. Good, bad, or ugly. Before I was doin' da ugly part. Now, I am lookin' at da future wide-eyed.

We can do so much stuff as a family. I can't wait till my time is up and I can come back home. Dere's so much ta tell ya. Love, Daddy

Kaylee danced around the kitchen happily as her mother read the letters. They wanted him to come home now because he sounded so different than before.

Betsy and the children, except for Kaylee who could not write yet, wrote back every week. Kaylee always drew a picture for him, and it made Thomas laugh when he saw it.

The letters always packed the pages with happenings in the home and words of love and well wishes for him.

Dear Thomas: It was good to hear from ya. I miss ya so much, but you are where ya need to be right now... Love, Betsy

Thomas's heart felt a stirring that laid dormant for years. *Love.* He read Betsy's letters repeatedly, then folded them gently, and placed them in his drawer where his credentials and other treasures, including his GED certificate lay carefully wrapped to prevent them from destruction.

28 Christmas

One late fall afternoon while Betsy sipped tea, she glanced out the window as the dead leaves mixed with lazy snowflakes in the wind. Her eyes lifted to the unpainted barn fifty yards away. The tiny chickadees flew to the top and through the cracks in the ancient wooden boards. Generations of birds made their home here for the long wintertime and found lots of leftover hay seeds to peck.

Then, ideas whipped around inside Betsy's head like the leaves which blew about outside her window. Her tea grew cold as she drifted off into her deep thoughts. *What if? Is it possible?*

She jumped in her car and raced across town to the Johnson home. "I got dis idee. What if 'n we did somethin' different for Christmas dis year?" Her hands wildly gestured, and she talked as fast as an auctioneer.

When she paused, Deborah hugged Betsy. "That's amazing." The dining room table became an idea board filled with hurriedly scrawled notes and rough sketches.

Within days, gossip spread like measles in a country school. Calendars had a bright red circle around

December twenty-fourth. Notes read, **Christmas Eve Pageant at the Freeman Farm.**

It wasn't long until the good-natured bantering of the contractors echoed in the night air as they shored up the barn. While they worked inside, electricians labored outside to run electric lines and set up an outdoor display. When they were through, they yelled, "Let there be light!"

Suddenly, an explosion of colors drew the Freeman kids to the windows. Kaylee raced into the kitchen. "Mama, look at da purty lights." If the house were a ship, it would have capsized because every window on the side had people peering at the beautiful colors dancing and twirling on the white sparkly snow.

Giggles reverberated from Betsy's kitchen. Cookies popped out of the oven every ten minutes. Her counters groaned under the weight of the baked goods. The aroma drew the men inside to sample the wares.

Betsy laughed at them. "If ya don't stay out of da cookies dere won't be enough for da pageant. Now, shoo. Let us woman folk get our work done."

The teenagers and children, under the capable direction of dear old Miz Alma Pennington, practiced the pageant nightly. She thumped her cane hard on the floor when the youngsters got out of line. "Now you listen here, we are celebratin' the birth of our Lord. No more nonsense."

After the men declared that the barn was safe, the women arrived every day to clean out a generation's worth of cobwebs, dirt, and loose hay out of the main floor of the barn.

Then came the decorations. Hundreds of tiny lights, wrapped in garlands of holly and ivy, flickered around the perimeter of the main floor, turning the mundane barn into a sparkling winter wonderland. The Christmas tree in the corner, which was the largest in the county, lent the scent of pungent pine to the heavy aroma of cinnamon and spice.

A gazillion headlights poked through the darkness on December twenty-fourth as vehicles formed a long queue entering the Freeman Farm driveway. Joseph and Peter, along with Bailiff Simpson, and other officers directed the cars to park in neat rows. Meanwhile, the girls, Mrs. Hudson, and a group of volunteers from the soup kitchen offered each guest a cookie and a cup of hot chocolate or spiced cider. Shouts rang through the night. "We need more cookies." The girls scurried to the kitchen to refill the trays and thermoses. The scent of spices escaped into the air making a welcoming ambience to the festive crowd.

When starting time came, Betsy Freeman stood, walked to the front, and gave her loudest earsplitting whistle. Conversations ceased as people scattered like loose spray in the wind.

"Hey, everybody! Thank ya for comin'. Welcome ta da pageant. Thank ya for bein' dere when we needed ya most. It meant so much ta my kids and me. What better time dan Christmas ta show our thanks ta ev'ryone?"

She stepped aside as Pastor Johnson walked to the stage. "Father, thank you for what You have done for the Freemans."

"Amen," yelled Betsy.

Pastor Johnson ended his prayer and stepped aside. Miz Pennington hobbled up and took the microphone. "Shall we begin?"

Betsy glowed with happiness. A man's voice startled her. "Is dis seat taken?"

"Thomas!" She squealed joyously, and hugged him, then smothered him in kisses. I'm so glad da judge let ya come."

"Betsy, please, people are watchin'." Thomas blushed.

"I don't care. I'm over da moon."

Applause erupted like a clap of thunder in the packed-out barn.

"Now, shall we begin?" Miz Pennington brought the crowd to order.

"Not yet," came a woman's voice from the shadows in the back of the barn. Heads turned around. *Sproing! Creak! Pop!* It sounded like a rice cereal advertisement.

As soon as she stepped into the light, Thomas jumped from his seat like his pants were on fire, and raced back the aisle as if he was shot from a cannon. He grabbed the woman in a bear hug. "Mama! I've missed ya so much, but we can catch up later. Come up ta our seat. Dere's lotsa room." Together, arm-in-arm, they walked down the aisle.

The light filtering through the hay and dust in the air seemed to add a little sparkle of Christmas magic pregnant with meaning for the Freemans and all who knew the journey they had been on during the past year.

Finally, it was time to start. A tiny preschool boy stepped up on the makeshift platform and yelled out, "This is how it all went down!" He jumped off the stage and ran to his mother beaming with pride.

Spotlights from the loft illuminated Jenny Freeman as she walked onto the stage and read the Scriptures.

Luke 2:1-3

1.In those days a decree went out from Caesar Augustus that all the world should be registered.

2.This was the first registration when Quirinius was governor of Syria.

3.And all went to be registered, each to his own town. 7.

A commotion interrupted her reading. From the back of the barn came Farmer Whitehall leading a donkey while Hailey rode sidesaddle on it. "Let's just skip ta da juicy stuff," he said as he stepped into the spotlight. The audience erupted with laughter. As they approached the front where the makeshift stable was set up, Mary (Hailey) slid down wrapping her arms around her stomach. She and Farmer Whitehall took their place in the living nativity.

Jenny continued to read the Scripture.

Luke 2:6,7

6. And while they were there, the time came for her to give birth.

7. And she gave birth to her firstborn son and wrapped him in swaddling clothes and laid him in a manger, because there was no place for them in the inn.8.

With a deft shake of her robe, Hailey delivered her baby doll into the manger. Something rustled in the hay. As she looked down, she shrieked a blood-curdling scream, and Buttercup, Peter's calf, let out her loudest bellow from the stall across the barn.

"Well now," Farmer Whitehall drawled, "if'n dat ain't somethin'. A dog in da manger with, let's see..." He held up each puppy as the children counted, "One, two, three..." all the way to seven.

"So, if'n my figures are right, we got us seven li'l pups, and a mama all safe in the warm manger. Whadd'ya think of dat?"

"Mooo," Buttercup answered.

Chaos reigned as children rushed from every corner of the barn to see the puppies. At that moment, the shepherds led by Peter Freeman, hurried in from the freezing weather and knelt beside the manger.

Miz Pennington grabbed the microphone. "Awright, everybody. Settle down. After the pageant is over, you can come to see the dogs." She thumped her cane. The children's choir quickly sang, "Away in a Manger."

Finally, the teen chorus sang, "O Come, Let Us Adore Him." The accompanists had to adjust their timing to sixteenth notes instead of the quarter ones written on the music sheets.

When the last warbled notes finished echoing throughout the barn, Kaylee Freeman climbed up on the platform and held the microphone up to her mouth. "God bless us, everyone!"

The audience applauded loudly as she walked down the steps and ran across the room to crawl up in her mother's lap. That night had written itself in the town's history books as the best Christmas pageant ever.

~

After a lot of the joyous guests left and the clean-up crew was still doing last-minute work, Bobby, Freeman's neighbor, walked into the barn. Joseph spotted him and marched over angrily. "You're not s'posed to be here! Ya need to leave before dere's trouble."

"I didn't come to cause any problems. I'm lookin' for my dog, Lucy."

"She's in da manger."

"Wait. What's she doin' dere?"

"She had seven puppies last night, so she sought out the best place to bring her family into the world. The children loved them. OOHs, and AWWWs and squeals of delight filled the air. They were as excited to see them as they were for Christmas Day tomorrow."

Bobby approached and peered into the manger. When he saw the doll representing for baby Jesus, he paused, then squirmed. Tears started their trail down his cheeks.

"Ya cryin', Bobby?"

"Naw, it's da old dusty hay."

Joseph wasn't buying it. He had been where Bobby was at this minute and understood his uneasiness.

Finally, after a long silence, Bobby spoke, trying to throw Joseph off his track. "What was goin' on to'nite? Dere were billions of cars parked all over yer land."

"Didn't ya know? It was the Christmas Eve Pageant."

Bobby fidgeted. "I ain't never been to one of dose. What did ya do?"

"We had a retellin' of Jesus' birth. Do ya know who He is?"

Bobby shook his head.

In the flickering lights of the barn, sitting around the manger, Joseph and Bobby talked long into the night about Jesus, the Messiah. Joseph's face glowed when he shared his journey to find the Savior. "I used to hate my dad, but I learned ta forgive. I now love him and others around me."

Intrigued, Bobby asked, "Where do I start?"

As Pastor Johnson showed him to do, Joseph explained the Scriptures from his new Bible. Once Bobby understood, they bowed their heads, and Joseph helped him to pray for Jesus to come into his life too.

That night, a new star twinkled in the midnight sky as a newborn lamb (Bobby) was born into the Kingdom of God. It is what Christmas is all about.

29 Epilogue

Dear Betsy: How ya doin'? Since I ain't been drinkin', my mind is clear as a bell. Slowly, I've been cleanin' up my act in other ways, too. Since bein' here at Brock's Home, I think a lot, 'specially at night. Dose terrible things I done haunt me like a hound dog on a hunt. Dey come in my dreams and wake me up sweatin' and shakin'. Den, I think bout what God's doin' in my life. My thoughts change to thinkin' bout home, and ya, my Betsy girl. Ya done blew my socks clean off over Christmas, if'n I'd been wearin' any. How could you still love an ornery old polecat like me all dese years? Whoee! Girl! But my, oh my! Ya changed so much. Ya really do forgive, Betsy, ya live it. After all da stuff I done, ya just don't blame me anymore. I ain't heard swear words from yer mouth da whole time on Christmas Day. Ya handled da kids in a better way, and dey listened to ya so good.

Bein' away from ya is drivin' me crazy. In two weeks, we'll be together again for good. I'm worried a little bit bout comin' back home. Da kids may not be as forgivin' as ya are. Hailey stayed away from me all day. Joseph was friendly, but distant. Peter was more excited bout his calf den seein' me. Jenny and Kaylee didn't welcome me with open arms either. What's with dose kids? Was I dat bad of a dad?

I don't never wanna go away from ya. All I gotta do is stay away from da drinkin'. I can't do it on my own. I know dat with God's help and yers, I can stay clean and keep out of da slammer. Dere's better days ahead if'n we just hang on.

I'm doin' good at work. Bought me a purty blue four-wheel-drive truck with a 350 engine, overhead cams, and straight pipes so loud dey'll think Gabriel is blowin' his horn. Dis old girl goes just like da car we had when courtin'. Remember how when I floored it and whipped da handbrake, and ya slid over? Yep. I'm ready for some of dat magic again. I can't wait to take ya for a ride in Daddy's li'l farm truck down da Old Creek Road, just like old times. Love 4ever, Thomas.

~

Dear Thomas: So happy ta hear from ya. Yes, I remember dat old car and da Old Creek Road. Seems like every time we snuck away, we'd end up with another baby. Well, dis time it wasn't da Old Creek Road, but da time we spent together on Christmas.

I've been sicker dan a yeller dog, so I went ta da doc yesterday. Just wanna be sure of what was happenin'. Dey showed me on da screen dat a new little Freeman is growin' in my tummy. Couldn't believe it. At my age. Being a mom again. I ain't told anybody. Dis one is not gonna know da hittin' and screamin' from before. He or she (too early ta tell) will come ta a better house and get a proper raisin' from his or her mama and daddy. Can't wait til ya come home. I'm so proud of ya for stickin' it out and gettin' better. Love, Betsy (and baby) Shhh!

~

Betsy lay on the couch napping. Being pregnant wore her out. She had just dozed off when she thought she heard a knock on the door. She sat up. *There it was again. Hope it's not a salesperson. I don't want anything, and I'll send him packin' faster dan a cheetah chasin' a jackrabbit.* She undid the bolt lock, the chain, and the door lock, then opened it a crack.

"Can I come in?" the familiar voice asked.

"Of course, Thomas." She unlocked the screen door and swung it wide open. "Hi." She smothered him in kisses. They held each other in a long embrace.

"It's so good ta be home." Thomas grinned. When they stepped inside the door, he placed his hand on her swollen stomach. "Won't be long til others'll be askin' questions."

"I know, but da kids and yer mom need ta know first. I was waitin' til ya got home. We can tell dem tonight at supper."

They sat cuddled up on the couch, quietly basking in being together again. Betsy knew that Thomas would need to get out into the greenhouses soon because Spring was right around the corner. That meant sowing the seeds, so there would be profit at harvesttime.

"It so good ta have ya by my side." Betsy reached over and grabbed his hand.

"Hmm hmmm."

"Take time ta be with da kiddos tonight, den tomorrow ya can be bright-eyed, and bushy tailed. Dey missed ya as much as I did."

Thomas looked around. "Betsy, you're keepin' a fine house. Ya could eat off da floor. "

Not used to compliments from him, Betsy blushed.

"Da kids help me a lot."

It wasn't long before the children burst through the door. "Daddy," Kaylee squealed, hopped up on his lap, and wrapped her arms around his neck.

The next hour flew by as Peter showed off his calf, Buttercup. The older ones only offered fist bumps and smiled weakly. *"It looks like I have my work cut out for me. I wronged dem, and now I gotta pay da piper, but I got all da time in da world ta make up with dem.* Regret flashed across his mind. *I need ta do betta and prove myself.*

He didn't have long to think those thoughts because Betsy announced. "Supper will be ready in five minutes." The children rushed off to wash their hands and faces, then comb their hair. That is one thing that they remembered from their time with Mrs. Baker.

Once they were all seated, they bowed their heads for grace. Once they said "Amen," they avoided grabbing, slopping, or spilling the food. The bowls and platters went around the table carefully and ended up on the sidebar. No one shouted or screamed.

Betsy cleared her throat. "We got somethin' ta say." You could've heard a pin drop as silence came over the table. All eyes turned to her as she announced, "Y'all are gonna get a brother or sister."

"Dat ain't fair. I'm da baby of da family." Kaylee pouted.

"Sorry, honey. You'll love da new baby when he or she arrives." Betsy tried to console her daughter. *Dis'll be good for her. She's a bit spoilt. I'm gonna need ta work with her ta help her adjust.*

After a moment of shocked surprise, the children talked all at once. Betsy and Thomas ignored them.

This was their moment; she winked at Thomas. He made a secret gesture, and she blushed.

~

The next morning when Caroline arrived to get the children ready for school, she saw an unfamiliar truck in the driveway. She cautiously approached the house and knocked on the door. She squealed happily when Thomas opened it and switched on the porch light.

He stepped into the pre-dawn darkness and squinted through the blackness. He caught sight of a familiar face.

"Mama!" Thomas wrapped his arms around her. "I'm so glad to see you."

"And me too. It's been so long…" Her words trailed off.

"What are ya doin' here at dis hour of da mornin'? Da birds ain't even singin' yet?"

"I see to it that the children get to the school bus on time. Betsy and I worked out this system, and it goes smoothly."

"Well, come in." Thomas stepped out of the doorway. "I wasn't sure how to do da girls' hair. Peter is up already, and out at the barn feedin' his calf and some stray animals he's found. If'n it's all da same to ya, I gotta get back to work in da greenhouse."

"No problem. It's so nice to see you. I'll take care of the girls for you."

"Thanks." Thomas turned and walked toward the newly erected building fifty feet away.

The relationships within the Freeman family began to change. Where there was shouting and cursing before, now there were sounds of silence inside, and happy shouts as the children played outside on the equipment that Thomas installed for them.

He did his best to make up time with all his children. Daily, the kids attitudes toward their dad began to soften. Joseph and Hailey were more receptive to his advice. Thomas had failed them miserably in their earlier years, but now they were in a new chapter as a family.

Thomas stepped up to the plate alongside his wife. He cared for her needs better than he did when she was expecting her other children. Now, he doted on her with tenderness instead of his fists. Those days were gone.

Months passed, and Fall arrived. The long-awaited bundle of joy was about to make an entrance. When the arduous work of labor was over, Betsy held little Grace in her arms. She looked toward the Heavens. *"Thank ya, God way up in da sky, for dis li'l girl."*

When Betsy was able to go back to church, the family car eased into the parking lot and stopped gently. Joseph jumped out of the driver's seat, opened his siblings' door, and unhooked little Grace from her car seat. He turned and handed her to Betsy. Kaylee and Jenny held their daddy's hands as they skipped happily to the church doors. Hailey lumbered along with the massive diaper bag slung over her shoulder. Peter joined the march with slicked-back hair and a brown suit. He was growing into a fine young man.

When the Freeman family entered the foyer, they greeted the pastor. People rushed forward to see the baby. Thomas took his new daughter from Betsy and held her up. "This is Grace."

That morning, flanked by her siblings, parents, Miz Pennington, and Caroline Freeman, Pastor Johnson held the baby in his arms. "Today, O Lord, we lift to You Grace Lynnette Freeman. May this little one always be a reminder of Your grace…the unmerited favor of God."

About the Author

Over the course of authoring this book, I began to see my world in a unique way. I grew up in a poverty-stricken region of Central Pennsylvania. The coal and lumber industries had long since dwindled. As we say in the Appalachian Mountains, it was a hard scrabble way of life for me and my seven siblings. There were many times we would go hunting and foraging for food, so we could survive.

At twelve years of age, I began babysitting and doing odd jobs to buy my own clothes and personal supplies. I learned at an early age the value of hard work. The "make-do" mindset was built into the fiber of an Appalachian woman.

I excelled in Language arts from elementary age to college. Even as a young girl, I was found with a notebook, drafting short stories, essays, poems, and other pieces of literature.

As time went on, I attended college where I met my husband, David, who worked on campus for a missions' organization. He has been the greatest critic and support for many years. We raised our two sons together. They were surrounded by piles of printer paper as I continually wrote Christmas and Easter programs, devotionals, and other works, some of which are available through www.Amazon.com.

Several years ago, I joined Word Weavers International. The critique group encouraged me in many ways to develop the short story, *We Stand Together,* into far more polished form you read today.

The Taming of the Rude is my debut novel. My goal has always been to offer hope to the hurting. From my proceeds, I do things, like offering gift baskets for the holidays, giving to a mission's project, etc.

Look for two upcoming books in the Community Church Series.
The Little Girl in the Brown Dress (Prequel)
How Could You? (Sequel)

Acknowledgments

A person does not write alone. A good writer pulls from their wealth of friendships, experiences, and groups they are a part of.

My greatest inspiration was the Creator Himself. He gave me the drive and connections to make this six-year journey possible.

I've authored many shorter stories and self-published most of them with the help of my husband and sons as sounding boards. In this work, my son Bradley collaborated with me to help shape the characters into what they became.

Word Weavers, International Page 26 leader, Diane Tatum, beta read and encouraged me to be the best I can be. I've grown so much as a writer from our critique group.

Bibliography

E-sword, 2018, Rick Meyers. All Scriptures are English Standard Version of the Holy Bible.

1.   James 1:3
2.   James 1:23-34
3.   James 1:19
4.   2 Kings 16:20
5.   Matthew 6:14,15
6.   Matthew 22:39
7.   Luke 2:1-3
8.   Luke 2:6,7

Other Works by this Author

Amazon Books, Devotionals
Mrs. Murphy's Christmas Tree ASIN : B07KCNL6J6
Christmas Moments with the Prophets   B07DPCNDNK
Digging Up Pearls   B07H5DSHSN
Journey to Easter   B06X6CTS41

Coming Soon
The Little Girl in the Brown Dress
How Could You?